Hartley,

with every blessing

28/7/22

COLIN RANK

# WORDS IN RED

Evidence for the Prosecution

novum premium

This book is also
available as
e-book.

www.novum-publishing.co.uk

© 2022 novum publishing

ISBN 978-3-99130-094-6
Editing: Ashleigh Brassfield, DipEdit
Cover photo:
Pamela Mcadams | Dreamstime.com
Cover design, layout & typesetting:
novum publishing
Internal illustration: Colin Rank

**www.novum-publishing.co.uk**

**Climate neutral**
Print product
ClimatePartner.com/16547-2201-1002

PART 1
# THE TRAP

*"It's not what you look at that matters, it's what you see."*
Henry David Thoreau

# Chapter 1

# COMPROMISED

It had been a perfect summer's day. The sun was gently descending behind the Judean hills, casting three long shadows across Jerusalem from the three magnificent towers that ascended out of the citadel next to King Herod's Palace, with the Phasael Tower dominating the other two.

The evening sunset flooded across the dolomite limestone city, painting the western walls of Herod's magnificent Temple in a wonderful golden orange light.

Simon Ish Kerioth[1], a scribe in his mid-forties, had spent the day at work making copy scrolls of the Psalms for his old friend Rabbi Nathan from Nazareth.

Now at the end of the day, he stood back from the scroll he had been working on and wandered over to the window. His back ached from standing, as was customary when reading or writing scripture. With his ink-stained hands resting on the sill, he gazed north out of the open window of the Old Refectory, taking in the tranquil scene. The Old Refectory was part of a disused community building and had been converted to a studio for scribes working on manuscripts. It was located close to the High Priest's house and was brought into use during the reconstruction of the Temple workshops. When the reconstruction work was complete and most of the Scribes had returned, the High Priest at the time had permitted Simon to remain there on his own. He was quite a solitary individual and the privacy it afforded for his work appealed to him. From his vantage point he had a clear view of Herod's palace on his left and the great, refurbished, gleaming Herodian Temple on the right.

Standing at the window looking out across Jerusalem, the same evening light gently painted his white robes and tinged his grey beard a glorious rose pink.

He breathed in the early evening air. A fragrance of spices from the old marketplace below mixed with the scent of fresh blooms.

It was a truly glorious evening, and as he stood there taking in the spectacle and listening to the sound of the evening bustle in Jerusalem, he felt very much at peace.

He closed the wooden shutters, rolled up his work and tidied up his workplace, closing with a traditional prayer to finish off the day before making his way downstairs and out onto the street. Enjoying a continuing sense of well-being, he made his way slowly through the small square opposite his home.

Suddenly, without any warning, a young man barged into him, brushing his arm with such force that it was all he could do to stay upright. The young man glanced back only briefly to check if he was still standing. Simon recognised him as a runner for the High Priest Caiaphas.

'Why don't you mind where you're going?' He shouted out after the boy, but the lad took no notice.

Simon climbed the semi-circular steps to the entrance of his lodgings and was greeted cheerily by Anna the housekeeper. He felt thoroughly put out by the incident in the square. It had utterly ruined his evening. He gruffly mumbled a greeting to her as he climbed the stairs to his apartment on the third floor. Anna knew his mood swings were only temporary and that when he was upset about something he was best left alone.

Feeling his way down the dark corridor leading to his rooms, he lifted the door latch and entered.

There on the floor, slipped under the door, a folded parchment note was awaiting him in the half light. He picked it up and turned it over. There was a seal on the back, but it was too dark to read it. Picking up his oil lamp, he retraced his steps to the pilot light on the window sill at the top of the stairs and lit the little oil lamp. He then saw that the seal was that of the High Priest, Caiaphas.

As he returned down the eerily dark passageway, to his horror, he was shocked at the sight of a menacing looking figure lurking in the darkness just beyond his door. It made him jump and he stepped backwards catching his breath. He must have walked right past him in the darkness.

'What do you want?' he enquired nervously. The man approached as Simon backed away. The faint light from the lamp illuminated his face and he could see that it was the lad who had nearly knocked him over earlier. 'You half frightened me to death, young man! What do you mean by lurking in the dark back there?'

'I'm sorry, sir. I have orders to escort you to the High Priest. I thought it best for you to read the message first, sir.'

Simon re-entered his apartment. 'I see, so why all the urgency?'

'I don't know, sir. I'm just here to escort you immediately to His Holiness.'

Simon looked at the young man. He was well built, and his frame filled the doorway. His dark eyes fixed the older man with a brazen stare.

Simon opened the note. It was indeed a summons from the High Priest.

'Very well, but let me first wash. It's been a hot day and I have ink on my hands. Wait there while I prepare myself.' Simon made to close the door, but the young man moved forward into the doorway. He stood there blocking the way. Simon backed away nervously.

What was all this about? Did the High Priest suspect he was allowing his old friend Rabbi Nathan to jump the queue for a fee? Everyone knew that sort of thing went on. Surely, he wouldn't make an issue out of something so petty. It was hard enough for a scribe to make ends meet in Jerusalem. But then Caiaphas could be extremely unpredictable.

Deliberately stalling for time to think, he poured some water into a bowl and, using a small piece of pumice stone, he slowly rubbed off the ink stains.

He felt his stomach turn at the thought of a late-night audience with the High Priest; he was well known for his volatile temper.

The two men made their way down the corridor and out into the street without speaking a word. The light was fading fast as they crossed the little square towards the High Priest's residence.

On reaching the Gate House the young man ordered the guard to open the door.

From there they followed the covered walkway through a series of carved stone archways to a small side entrance, where they were met by the night guard with a lamp. He dismissed the runner and took Simon up a stone spiral staircase and along a wide corridor, then through two large oak doors. Once inside he was shown into a small anteroom. The guard knocked on the door and waited.

'Come!' A voice commanded them to enter, and the guard retired to a position outside.

The room was spacious and well-lit by numerous oil lamps. A personal servant stood on one side of the room. On the far side a small man dressed in a white tunic with matching headdress was seated behind a large desk piled high with scrolls. Caiaphas, the High Priest, stood up and came around the front of the desk. He gestured to Simon to sit down on some loose cushions on the floor next to a couple of small decorative tables.

Simon bowed to the High Priest before taking a seat as requested. He waited to be addressed.

'Would you care for a cup of wine, Simon?' the High Priest asked, gesturing to the servant. Simon remained silent. This was not an invitation; it was an instruction. The two men knew that by drinking together they were entering a covenant of confidentiality. The servant filled two silver cups which he proceeded to serve.

'That will be all for tonight.' Caiaphas motioned to the servant to retire.

Caiaphas blessed the wine and both men drank.

'I have brought you here to discuss a matter of great importance.' The High Priest smiled faintly. 'I'll get straight to the point, Simon.' He put his cup down. 'You see; I want you to gather some information for me on a man who is posing a significant threat to our entire nation. You will recall your part in collecting some useful evidence on John the Baptist?' He paused before continuing casually, 'As it happens, that information was overtaken by events, but now there is a new and much more dangerous threat from a man they call Yeshua the Nazarene. He is a much greater threat than John. We know they are related, but I believe that together they may have a more sinister purpose.

'There are reports that this Yeshua is already teaching about the establishment of a new Kingdom. This is the sort of talk that is not only dangerous for Israel but will reverberate all the way back to Rome! It's a serious threat to everything we've worked for and must be stopped!'

Caiaphas thumped the palm of his hand with a clenched fist before composing himself and reaching for his cup of wine. Clearly the subject got under his skin. He took a sip while studying Simon over the rim. The dim light of the oil lamps was enough to betray his ugly mood. Simon swallowed nervously, the pit of his stomach recoiling. This sort of outburst was precisely what he had feared.

This was a project that Simon wanted to avoid at all costs. Like everyone else, he had heard about Yeshua, but he was in the middle of making a copy of the Psalms for Rabbi Nathan, from whom he had already taken a sizeable deposit. He also hated travelling. The thought of following this Yeshua character through the Galilean countryside and staying in all those hostels crawling with bed bugs filled him with disgust. He didn't much care for Galilee or the Galileans if the truth were known. Above all, he wanted to avoid getting embroiled in a potentially trumped-up case which, if it went against Caiaphas, would end up being his fault.

'Your Holiness,' Simon interjected, 'I have heard it reported that this man is surrounded by a fairly rough bunch of local Galileans who are supposed to be his disciples, but no doubt they are there to protect him. I'm no longer a young man, Your Holiness. I am sure this task is better suited to a more able-bodied person than

I. And, what's more, he may prove much more difficult to get close to than John the Baptist. I'm not at all sure I'd be the best person to do that. Indeed. I have heard he is quite hostile to anyone associated with the Scribes and Pharisees.'

The High Priest rose to his feet, cup in hand and walked slowly over to the open window. He closed the shutters before crossing the room, opening the door, and dismissing the duty guard.

Caiaphas casually sat down again, gently replacing his cup on the small side table. The change in his demeanour frightened Simon.

He leant forward menacingly; his ugly expression illuminated by the light of an oil lamp. Simon had a bad feeling about what might be coming next.

Then quite casually he said, 'I think your son might help you get close to him.' He sat back watching Simon closely.

Simon's heart was pounding in his chest.

'What son, Your Holiness?' he asked trying to control his voice.

'Judas.' The High Priest responded, adding pointedly. 'Judas Ish Kerioth.'

Simon was dumfounded. How on earth could he possibly know about Judas? Even Judas didn't know the true identity of his father.

The affair with Judas' mother had been very brief – a huge mistake which had threatened to ruin Simon's career at the time. If it became known that he had an illegitimate son his position as a scribe would be over! He would be ruined.

He tried to compose himself.

'I am afraid I don't know what you're referring to, Your Holiness. I have a nephew called Judas, but he is not my son. I do not have a son. I am celibate and always have been...'

The High Priest cut in, reaching for his wine cup. 'I can't disclose my sources, but they are entirely reliable. Miriam was a married woman, married to your brother in fact, and unfortunately you didn't know that it was your brother who was incapable of having any children. You thought it was Miriam who was barren, and you took your chances.

'Look, I won't go into the details, it's late and I didn't bring you here to incriminate you, but I know the whole sordid story and I know you've taken an interest in the boy since he was small and grew up with your family.

'And I also know about what happened to your brother Alexander, when he found out about Judas a few years later. At the time Miriam was pregnant, and he was up here in Jerusalem. You thought that you had got away with it, but walls have ears, Simon, and he found out. It's a pity Alexander's body was found dead in a dark alley shortly after he found out, don't you think? I wonder who killed him? I don't suppose you know do you?'

Simon was speechless. He could feel the blood draining out of his face.

'You're a piece of excrement, Simon Ish Kerioth! But even excrement has its uses!' Caiaphas glared at him.

'Well, don't you have anything to say for yourself?' Caiaphas paused, 'I suppose not. So – this is what you're going to do,' he said, getting up and returning to his desk and rummaging about in a drawer. 'You're going to drop everything including your project for Rabbi Nathan in Nazareth – yes, I know all about that too – and you'll set off for the Galilee tomorrow. The man Yeshua and his band of followers were last seen operating out of Capernaum. He's staying in a house belonging to the mother-in-law of one of them. He's called Simon and he's a fisherman. Ah, here we are.' Caiaphas closed the drawer and straightened up depositing a small purse on the desktop. 'Of the dozen he's selected to be his inner circle, many are related, so expect to come up against some opposition. As you know, blood's thicker than water. Judas will be your passport to get close to this traitor, and between the two of you I expect you to gather as much damning evidence as you can. Make sure you get it all down word for word. I don't want any slipups when we bring him to trial. Blasphemy, law breaking, you know the sort of things we need. We suspect he may be attempting to establish himself as a Messiah figure and you know how that would go down with the Romans.'

Simon felt a sense of panic rising up inside. 'I haven't seen Judas in a while. What if he doesn't recognise me?'

'If he's anything like you, Simon, he will be looking after the purse for the group and making a bit on the side!' Caiaphas chuckled. 'You gave him an education and looked after him whenever he was in need. I don't suppose he will have forgotten his old uncle, do you?'

With that he picked up the purse and tossed it to Simon over the desk.

'That's an advance to look after your expenses. I want a report every six weeks by courier and it better be good. Now get out of my sight!' he barked, getting up and crossing the room. He opened the door and peered into the darkness.

'Guard!' he yelled out.

Somewhere from down a dark corridor a man appeared.

'Show this man out.' Pointing to Simon's cup, he added, 'Oh and take that cup with you. I don't want it on the premises. It's tainted!'

'Thank you, Your Holiness,' replied the guard clutching the silver cup as he proceeded to escort Simon out into the night.

1 **Note:** Ish Kerioth, a man from Kerioth.

14

Chapter 2

# A FORGOTTEN PAST

Simon's head was spinning as he closed the door of his apartment that night. The small parchment note lay face down on his table, where he had left it a few hours before. He picked it up and re-read the summons. How on earth could Caiaphas have learnt about Miriam?

As he lay down on his bed, his thoughts returned to his sister-in-law, who had been living just a short distance away from his home in Kerioth about twenty-five miles south of Jerusalem. At the time he was just eighteen and studying to qualify for a place at the school of Gamaliel in Jerusalem. His elder brother, Alexander, had got married and settled in a house that had previously belonged to his great-grandfather.

His father John kept a flock of sheep and goats, which he tended in pastures near their home, and Alexander, who traded in asphalt from the Dead Sea, spent long periods away from home on business. While he was away Miriam would often lodge with the family. He and Miriam had been married for over six years but had no children. Everyone assumed she was barren.

Miriam was four years older than Simon. She was fun and intelligent, had a lovely generous smile, and was quite tall with beautiful dark eyes and long, raven black hair. She was seventeen when she got married having lived with her elderly parents just inside Jerusalem. Her father knew John quite well and it was through that friendship that she had become betrothed to Alexander.

One summer while Alexander was away on an extended business trip to Spain, Simon had been in school next to the Synagogue doing an extra tutorial for an exam. His tutor had to leave early to attend an appointment with the Rabbi.

He made his way back home to find his mother Ruth out shopping at the market and his father still out in the field.

He went through to his room in the annexe where Miriam was staying. As he entered, he noticed the door to her bedroom was ajar and through the crack he caught sight of her washing her hair in a large bowl of water. She was stripped to the waist and had her back to the doorway. He stood there watching her for several minutes. She had a slim frame and a shaft of the evening light flickered through the tree outside her shuttered window and played on her naked breast.

He became fascinated with what he was seeing and just stood there.

Suddenly the back door opened with a noisy creak. It was Ruth, Simon's mother.

He turned to bolt into his room but as he reached his door he glanced back once more. She had half turned to see who was there and their eyes met for a fraction of a second before she reached out for a towel to cover herself up.

That night he lay awake. The image of Miriam was all he could think about. Her naked torso, arms raised as she poured water from a jug to rinse her long black hair and, as she did so, revealing the outline of her breast. The thought of her lying alone across the hall was utterly intoxicating.

The following day nothing was said, but over the next few days he found himself frequently glancing her way, and when their eyes met she would smile nervously and shyly look away. Daily he could feel himself regarding her in a way he had never felt before. He knew it was wrong, but somehow it didn't seem to matter anymore.

Then one evening he found himself once more dismissed from class early.

He raced home. Miriam was preparing some food in the kitchen. She was alone. She looked up at Simon and greeted him with a broad smile. He dumped his bag on the floor and moved slowly around the table to where she was standing, not really aware of what he was doing. His breathing quickened. He took hold of her hand, but she did not resist, and he began to lead her gently towards his room.

The next morning, they exchanged glances but nothing much was said. As he set off for school, he was overcome with disgust for what he had done. His mind flipped back and forth between the pleasure and the guilt. Miriam had clearly not resisted and had responded with pleasure. It would be his first and last experience. He knew he was not in love with Miriam. He was only too aware that his ambitions and his reputation could be utterly ruined by what he had done. The implications filled him with fear.

He felt very unsettled and disturbed and over the following days he became certain that he needed to take control of the situation and to get Miriam out of the house and to get away from her. He complained to his parents that he needed the room where she was staying for his further studies; for the scrolls which he had started to bring home from the library.

In the end she returned to her house of her own volition, sensing also a feeling of shame and fear should Alexander find out. She made an excuse, but Ruth had her suspicions, even if she kept them to herself. Something had happened, but she didn't know what; but Miriam had gone now, and things reverted to normal. Not a word was said.

Then, about two months later, Simon was returning home through the market when he saw Miriam looking at some fabrics. She hadn't seen him and he turned away pretending not to notice her. She had been waiting for him and left the stall and came towards him. Turning to see if she was still there he was taken aback to see her a few paces away and reaching into a pocket. She took out a small scrap of parchment which she pressed into his hand before moving away quickly without saying a word.

Simon didn't read it but stuffed it into his cloak pocket.

Once home he closed the door and took out the note. It said quite simply, "I think I'm having a baby."

Simon's heart nearly stopped. Surely that was impossible, since Miriam was unable to have children? Everyone said so. Then he thought to himself that it must be Alexander's, or maybe she was mistaken. Then he realised that Alexander had been away near-ly nine months and could not be the father. Perhaps she had had another illicit relationship. His head spun in panic. But what if she was pregnant and the baby was his?

He decided to speak to her as soon as possible, so the follow-ing evening he told his parents he was going to visit his friend Joel and then made his way to her house under cover of dusk. She opened the door and beckoned him in.

'What is this?' he whispered harshly, holding out the note. 'This has nothing to do with me! How can you be so sure you're having a baby anyway?'

An oil lamp on the side table bathed her beautiful face with a soft flattering light.

'Would you like a drink?' she asked in her gentle, kind voice.

But he didn't answer the question.

He looked at her and as he did so he felt those awful conflict-ing feelings flooding back. His look said it all.

Then reason returned to him.

It was her fault that they were in this mess! If she hadn't egged him on this would never have happened and in his confusion, he tried to justify himself.

'You will have to have the baby here,' he said, clutching his brow as if thinking hard. 'Then we can think about what we do.' His mind was all over the place. 'No, if Alexander finds out he will divorce you and then the whole family will be disgraced.'

Miriam's face began to show the stress and tears began to well up in her eyes.

'What am I going to do?' she sobbed. 'I thought I couldn't have children.'

'I don't know. I'll think of something. Perhaps you can give the baby away. Maybe to someone who has just lost a child.' he suggested.

'No!' pleaded Miriam as she dropped down on her knees. 'No, please…Alexander…' but before she could finish the door swung open and in walked Ruth.

'Simon?' she exclaimed in surprise. 'What are you doing here? I thought you said you were going over to see Joel.' She paused looking first at Miriam, who had stood up by now, and then back at her son, Simon.

Simon broke the silence. 'I can explain everything, mother.' But, of course, he couldn't. 'I was just bringing her some raisins which I bought in the market today.' And he picked up a small bowl of raisins sitting on the table and held it out. He was clutching at straws.

'Don't lie to me!' shouted Ruth. Then she noticed the small scrap of parchment on the floor and bent down to pick it up. She moved towards the lamp. Simon snatched it away, but not before she had read it.

'So that's what this is all about. You little slut!" she rounded on Miriam.

'No, mother!' pleaded Simon. 'It's all my fault,' he said, looking down at the floor in shame.

'You mean you raped her?' Asked Ruth.

'No, it wasn't like that. I took advantage of her,' he replied.

'More like she took advantage of you, you mean! I know your sort. Came to our house, took advantage of our kindness, and then thought you'd have a bit of fun on the side! Serves you right, you little whore!'

Miriam said nothing but buried her head in her hands, sobbing loudly.

'Shame on you!' shouted Ruth. 'And now I suppose you want money to keep him quiet?' she taunted.

'No! No! No! I just don't know what to do!' Miriam sank to her knees, sobbing uncontrollably.

Ruth fell silent as Simon watched hopelessly. She needed a plan to get them out of this mess.

She looked at Miriam and then back at Simon. Then her mood changed.

She knew Alexander had written to say he was returning soon for a short visit before going up to Jerusalem for a while. What if Miriam was to conceal her pregnancy from him, and after he had gone away again, she would write and tell him the news that he was to be a father?

When the baby was born, she could remain hidden away at home for a further three months and he would be told it had arrived. That way he would have no reason to suspect that it was not his.

She sat Miriam down and they went through the whole idea. They all agreed it was the best solution.

So, Alexander returned and left again shortly afterwards. Miriam had her baby six months later and never left home for another three months.

The little boy was named Judas, after his great-grandfather, and grew up thinking Simon was his uncle. As far as Simon was concerned, only Miriam and his mother knew the truth. John, his father, never suspected anything or so they thought.

Chapter 3

# GALILEE

Simon woke up and, having dressed and eaten, he reluctantly prepared to depart for Galilee on the mission he had hoped to avoid. But he would go, because he was afraid of Caiaphas who had somehow found out about his past. How was a complete mystery, but now Simon found himself in a dangerous position. He had heard about Caiaphas' methods, but seeing it all face to face was not a pretty sight. None of it fitted with the sort of person you would expect to find in a High Priest; yet he was a very successful High Priest. The ruling Prefect, Pontius Pilate liked him because Caiaphas knew what was wanted and had demonstrated he could deliver. The Prefect wanted peace and order on his watch, and he wasn't interested in anything less.

Caiaphas had managed to maintain a sort of equilibrium between the hot headed nationalists on one hand, who wanted Roman blood and the restoration of an independent Israel, and the more traditional and Aristocratic Sadducees on the other, who enjoyed strong connections with the rulers of their day. The Sadducees didn't trust the ultra-religious Pharisees with their legal rules and regulations. Alongside sat the monastic Essenes, who held opposing views to just about everyone. They were obsessed with purity and inspired many with their apocalyptic teachings. As a group, the Essenes enjoyed widespread popular support through their schools and teachings. Embedded into all of these factions were the Scribes, whose simple devotion to the Holy Scriptures made them friends in almost all the other camps. They taught, translated, and provided the clerical services that made the whole system function. However, they all had one thing in common, which was a deep hatred and suspicion of the Romans: the occupying power.

Whether they appreciated it or not, all these factions made a good living out of the stability and financial input which the Roman Empire was providing. As ever, for those at the top the pickings were rich, but for those at the bottom, life was harsh.

Simon packed a few possessions into a bag which he slung over one shoulder. Over the other he carried his trusty leather document cylinder containing all his writing materials. He set off northwards for the Galilee. This was a journey he had made before, and he was acquainted with both the safest route and his favourite stops.

Not far from Jerusalem he joined up with a group of travellers who were heading in the same direction. He tagged along with them for company and, most importantly, for security.

He had plenty of time to think as he walked, and inevitably he began to think of seeing Judas again after so long. The last time he had seen him was in Batanea to the east of the Jordan River, where John the Baptist had been preaching to large crowds. The political climate there was relatively benign under Philip, Herod the Great's youngest son, and there was plenty of water for John's mass baptisms. John had a sort of magnetic influence over the people. His call to repentance had touched a nerve with many, including Judas, and he and his contemporaries had travelled there in search of this remarkable man.

Yeshua the Nazarene was not associated with John's ministry, although he was a cousin. The two men were very different. John had huge influence with the people and had attracted widespread popular support. In the tinder dry political climate where one spark could start a firestorm, the Roman authorities had sought assurances that no such firestorm would happen on their watch.

Simon had been sent to document John's activities and report back but there was widespread access to John, so the job was relatively easy, and he was able to reassure the leadership that he presented little threat to the authorities. His reports were being given directly to the Roman Prefect who treated them as valuable corroborative intelligence.

While Simon was there he had stumbled across Judas, who had taken a keen interest in seeking out anyone who he thought might lay claim to being the Messiah, the Anointed One. Everyone was anticipating the arrival of the Messiah, and John had made it very clear he himself was not the Messiah but that the Messiah was coming soon. All of this had fuelled a volatile expectation.

Philip's brother Herod Antipas had become embroiled in an incestuous marriage affair, which resulted in John the Baptist passing judgement on the matter. That upset Herod or, more particularly, his wife Herodias, who wanted revenge. As a result, John was imprisoned at Machaerus, a fortress on the north-eastern side of the Dead Sea. Herod found John intriguing and despite his incarceration he continued to summon him for lengthy discussions together. It was a curious relationship.

Simon remembered it all well because, on account of his assistance with intelligence gathering, he had been asked to represent Caiaphas alongside a wide-ranging group of military and other dignitaries at a banquet which Herod had put on for his birthday. Machaerus was an impressive fortress with a sumptuous palace.

As the wine and entertainment flowed Herodias had cunningly arranged for a dance to be performed for Herod by her very beautiful young daughter. Herod had made no secret of his admiration for her.

As the party was in full swing, Herodias leant across and whispered in her husband's ear that she had a special birthday treat for him. The King had consumed rather more wine than was good for him and when she asked the Master of Ceremonies to halt proceedings so that she could reveal her special treat, Herod could barely conceal his excitement.

A hush descended over the guests. Simon, who was reclining a short distance behind the Royal couple, had a clear view of what happened next.

The Master of Ceremonies stepped forward.

'Your Majesty,' he began bowing low before the King, 'Tonight to mark the occasion of your birthday and by special permission of Her Royal Highness, Queen Herodias, I introduce to you tonight's mystery guest performer.' He bowed low once more.

'Your Majesty, for your pleasure, I present to you, a Princess.' He drew out the introduction to full effect before sweeping into another low bow and retiring.

The musicians began to play very softly as a troupe of dancers slowly entered the stage from either side in front of the Royal couple. They proceeded to dance around the top table, collecting up the flaming torches which were illuminating the area. As they danced, two others brought a fine woven silk screen across the front of the stage. The music rose slowly in a crescendo of rhythm. Then the dancers moved gracefully behind the screen, placing the torches in a row of holders at the back of the stage, thus revealing its transparency. As they withdrew, the figure of a sole female dancer remained in silhouette, stretched out across the floor, head and arms reposed along an extended leg.

The music stopped with the crash of cymbals and as the sound decayed, a dark silence descended over the banqueting hall. Everyone strained to get a better view.

The screen drew back slowly to reveal the young girl motionless on the floor. The musicians played on softly.

The King immediately recognised the Queen's daughter and beamed with delight as she arose to dance for him. She was graceful and skilful, dressed in a translucent, full-length veiled dress of the finest silk from the Far East. As she danced, the King could clearly glimpse the outline of her beautiful figure silhouetted against the flames as she passed to and fro between him and the torches.

The murmurs and gasps of the guests rippled around the hall.

The King sat motionless, transfixed, his face softly lit by the flickering light as the young Princess twisted and turned to his unashamed and very evident pleasure. Her dance quickened into a frenzy of erotic movement, but the Queen saw nothing of it, her stony glare transfixing the King like a lioness about to pounce.

Finally, the Princess threw herself to the ground in a finale of surrender, sliding gracefully across the polished stone flagstones and coming to a halt right in front of the King.

She lay there motionless as the King rose to his feet accompanied by rapturous applause from the delighted guests. Even Simon found himself caught up in the exhilaration of her magnificent performance. He had never seen anything like it. Across the hall he could see the Queen's face and what he saw sent a shiver down his spine. A look of sheer evil spread across her face, and something told him that the performance was only just beginning.

As the applause subsided, the King congratulated the young girl, who had by now risen to her feet to acknowledge the applause. As she did so, he staggered to his feet and stepped up onto the low stage, taking her by the hand and showing her off to thunderous applause.

The king motioned with his hand and the hall fell silent.

'What can I say?' he asked almost speechless as he swayed unsteadily beside her. 'Name your pleasure, my dear, and I will grant it!' he slurred. 'No! I swear to you, ask of me whatever you want up to...' and he paused before blurting out defiantly, 'up to half my Kingdom!' The guests erupted in sheer delight.

As Simon watched the Queen, he was shocked to see her countenance transform from an evil stare into uncontrollable, triumphant laughter.

The young girl walked over to her mother to ask her advice.

'What shall I ask, Mother?' She enquired tentatively.

'Ask for...' the Queen paused making sure everyone was listening. 'Ask for the head of John the Baptist...' There was an audible gasp from the guests, followed by a silence that was so intense you could hear the torches hiss and roar in the darkness. Not one single guest dared to move. '...on a plate!' she added whimsically, her eyes locked on to her quarry.

Herod's face fell like a sack of wheat off the back of a cart. He realised he had just walked into one of Herodias' evil traps. He frantically looked around the hall. Distinguished guests returned his anguished gaze, but there was no way out and he knew it.

His inebriated head sagged wearily onto his chest and without even looking up he uttered the fatal words.

'Bring me the head of John the Baptist…on a plate.' he ordered in a low mumble.

Gasps rippled around the hall, but no one spoke a word.

Then, turning to Herodias, he bellowed out angrily, 'Let the party continue!' and then meekly repeating, 'Let the party continue.'

The musicians struck up and the waiters were hurriedly despatched to charge glasses and serve more food.

Herod Antipas held his wife's stare for a second before he slumped down on the cushions, his face a study of abject defeat.

Chapter 4

# CAPERNAUM

The journey for Simon had been dusty and painful as, three days later, he passed the Palace at Tiberias, home of Herod in the province of Galilee.

Capernaum was unusually quiet. This thriving olive oil producing community seemed almost deserted as he checked in to an Inn where he often stayed, just a stone's throw from the synagogue.

His feet were sore, and he asked the innkeeper if he could arrange for a foot massage. The innkeeper apologetically explained that half the town had gone off after a man called Yeshua from Nazareth, who had caused quite a stir locally by healing sick people without medicine and curing the demonically possessed with a single command. Only a few weeks before he himself had been in the synagogue when a man he knew quite well suddenly fell to the ground shouting out at Yeshua for no apparent reason. At the time all Yeshua had been doing was teaching the people. It was fascinating stuff, unlike anything he had heard before.

'Then suddenly this friend of mine started shouting at him, asking him what business he had with us. I couldn't make out quite why he was so upset. He was asking why Yeshua was going to destroy us. Anyway, he went on shouting at Yeshua in a most uncharacteristic way. Then he started saying that he knew who Yeshua was, and he accused him of being the Holy one of G_d. It made no sense to me at the time, but then Yeshua rounded on him quite angrily. He got right up close to my friend and said in a forceful way, "Shut up and come out!" and I suddenly understood what was happening. Then all hell broke loose. It was shocking to see my friend fall down and start thrashing about on the floor, screaming at Yeshua, who remained quite calm. Then all of a sudden he went all limp and just lay there still as if he was dead!' The innkeeper looked quite amazed at the recollection of it all before going on.

'Then Yeshua bent down and took him by the hand, and he got up and started talking in his usual manner. He spoke to my friend for some minutes before they left together.

'The place was in an uproar. Nothing like that has ever happened here to my knowledge. I knew this man! As far as I was concerned, he was an upright member of the synagogue. You would never have guessed he had anything like that the matter with him.

'Anyway, since then people have just downed tools and gone after him as if the end of the world had come.'

Simon listened intently. He took out a stylus and a wax tablet and made a few notes. The innkeeper went on.

'For a while Yeshua was staying down the road here, with Simon the Fisherman's mother-in-law, but within a day or so it was mayhem here. People came from all over the place bringing sick and incapacitated relatives for him to heal and the more he healed the more they brought! You simply couldn't move in town. I've never seen anything like it!' The innkeeper shook his head.

'Where is he now?' asked Simon.

'The last I heard he was teaching them all from a boat by the sea, just along the coast. But I've got a business to run so I'm the only one left round here...' his voice tailed off and he stood there staring at the floor. 'Maybe I should have gone out after him too,' he added ruefully.

It was getting late, so Simon resolved to try and find Yeshua and his followers the next day. Hopefully he would find Judas there as well.

In the morning he dropped in at the synagogue to see if he could find out the exact whereabouts of Yeshua. When he arrived, he got quite a frosty reception from the Rabbi. It soon became clear that he felt the people were being led astray. In fact, he didn't have a good word to say about it. When Simon asked him about the incident in the synagogue earlier, he became very defensive, dismissing it as something and nothing. He was adamant that he didn't have members of his synagogue who were 'demon possessed', whatever that meant.

'I agree with the Pharisees and Scribes who are up here from Jerusalem. They reckon this man Yeshua from Nazareth is doing his tricks of casting out demons by Beelzebul and that he is using demonic power to heal people.'

'Did they put that to him?' asked Simon.

'You will be able to ask them that yourself. They're due back here this morning. Apparently, this man Yeshua has invited them all to a gathering at the house where Simon the fisherman lives. He's agreed to address them in private.'

'So are you going?' asked Simon.

'Not if I can help it!' retorted the Rabbi. 'Why don't you go yourself and then you can make up your own mind?' He looked Simon up and down in his white robe. 'You're a scribe, aren't you? I am sure you will feel at home there. Now if you don't mind, I've got some work to get on with,' and looking up and down the empty streets, he added, 'I seem to be the only one round here who has. Good day to you, Sir!'

As Simon was returning to the inn, he became aware of the sound of a distant crowd, and looking up he could see a great cloud of dust blowing up the hillside. He assumed it must be Yeshua and his followers returning to town, so he hurried up to the inn and grabbed a book or two of wax tablets and a stylus. As he was going out through the lobby he bumped into the innkeeper.

'Where exactly is the house where Simon the fisherman lives?' he enquired.

'It's about halfway between the synagogue and the port on a little street called Fisherman's Lane, and it's the second house on the right. Shouldn't be difficult to find.'

Simon hurried off to find the house before the crowd arrived. He knocked at the door but there was no answer. He stepped back and as he looked up a young woman appeared at the upstairs window. He called up.

'Excuse me. Does Simon the fisherman live here? I'm trying to locate my nephew Judas from Kerioth.'

She had withdrawn into the house at this point but re-appeared. 'Did you say Judas Ish Kerioth?' she enquired. 'What business do you have with him?'

Simon thought for a moment.

'I'm his uncle and I have some important news for him.'

Simon waited as the woman disappeared once more and he could hear her coming downstairs. She unlocked the door and opened it a fraction.

'What news would that be?' She asked in her thick Galilean accent. 'Not that it's any of my business you understand.' Simon just about caught the gist of what she was saying.

'You must be Simon's wife,' he guessed, at which point she opened the door in surprise.

'Who's asking and how do you know who I am?' she asked.

'Let me introduce myself. I'm Simon, also from Kerioth.' And he held out his hand in greeting. 'I'm staying at the inn by the synagogue and I was hoping to find Judas…' his voice tailed off as he turned to see the crowd appearing at the end of the street opposite.

'You better come in before you get swept away by the crowd.' She opened the door and physically dragged Simon into the house slamming the door behind him.

'This is my mother. Mother, this is Simon, Judas' posh uncle. He's got a message for him.' She mentioned no names, so Simon was none the wiser who he was speaking to. He hadn't been called posh before, but clearly she felt his Judean accent warranted it.

'Would you like to wait in the back courtyard until they get here?' She showed Simon the door into a large, partly covered courtyard at the rear of the house and promptly shut the door as he went through.

The courtyard was covered by two high lean-to flat roofs sloping down from either side and supported by wooden pillars. At one end, large double doors led out into the street. The space in the middle was big enough to take a boat. The roofed area left a gap in the middle wide enough to have a small fire and to allow the rain to run off. The midday sun poured into the gap and provided some much-needed light. By the smell and various pieces of equipment lying around, the yard was obviously pur-pose built to store sailing and fishing equipment.

The lean-to roofs were constructed of reeds and mud clay to keep them waterproof. There were some crates and lots of old seat cushions off the boats scattered around the floor in antici-pation of the gathering.

It was no more than a few minutes before the crowd reached the house, and in walked a group of Pharisees and other scribes, looking a bit dazed and dusty from their journey. Seeing Simon, who some of them knew, they greeted him before sitting down. Meanwhile Simon's wife and mother-in-law, together with a group of other women, brought in a large pitcher of water and some cups on a tray, which they proceeded to serve to the assembled guests before retiring. Among the women who had entered with the rest of the group were some who were noticeably well dressed and well-spoken by comparison to the others. One in particular Simon recognised, but he couldn't quite place where he had seen her.

Some of the group he recognised as having been with John the Baptist beyond the Jordan River.

As they chatted, they told Simon about the remarkable things they had seen with Yeshua, and others shared their misgivings.

Just then, some other men dressed in local clothing whom he did not recognise filed in, followed by a tall man in a one-piece tunic who was clearly the man; Yeshua. He took up a po-sition next to the door and the assembled gathering drew up to hear what he had to say. Before he started, two others crept in, and Simon immediately recognised the one at the back as Judas.

There was still quite a noise coming from the crowd out-side, and Judas looked up nervously at the gap in the roof, but he hadn't noticed Simon.

Yeshua opened his arms and welcomed the gathering. No sooner had he opened his mouth than Simon saw for himself the extraordinary presence that he commanded. Every eye was fo-cussed on him, and every ear strained to hear what he was say-ing. His authority was tangible.

Simon had taken up a position opposite Yeshua at the back where he could see and hear. He took out his stylus and wax tablets. As he did so, Yeshua looked up at him and smiled as if he knew Simon. He then paused for a second, looking directly at Simon's hands, which were poised to write down anything which he thought would be useful evidence. As he did so, a strange sensation came over Simon. He suddenly found himself thinking about Moses, about to take down what G_d was telling him to write. The atmosphere caused the hairs to rise on the back of his neck and he felt a tingling sensation in his ears. He had never experienced such a sensation before, and it took him quite by surprise. It took a moment to recover his composure.

Meanwhile Yeshua had begun by refuting the suggestion that he cast out demons by the power of Beelzebub, a satanic prince of the underworld who was seen as Lord of all the flies, an insect despised for feeding on excrement. He dismissed their accusation saying that it made no sense, because a kingdom working against itself would never succeed. He went on to talk about forgiveness, that even those who blasphemed could be forgiven, but that blasphemy against the Holy Spirit could never be forgiven. Clearly, he was making a thinly veiled suggestion that their judgement put them in a very precarious position. They did not take kindly to his suggestion.

Simon carefully recorded his exact words as he spoke about forgiveness; statements which seemed to him to put Yeshua on a direct collision course with accepted law and practice and sounded as if he was accusing the Pharisees of committing an unforgivable sin. How outrageous!

As Yeshua spoke, he was frequently interrupted with questions from members of the audience. He was being challenged about his teaching on forgiveness. It seemed that he was implying that he had authority to act on G_d's behalf; that he had, in some way, a mission and a mandate to redeem the people of Israel.

John the Baptist had urged his followers to repent and be baptised, but it was always G_d who did the forgiving.

The debate was getting more and more heated. Tempers were frayed. Everyone was tired and hungry.

Then, just as the meeting was about to break up in chaos and disagreement, there was a commotion on the roof above where Yeshua was standing.

Four men had clambered up onto the roof, shouting and hacking away at the roof with their bare hands. Everyone's attention was distracted, so Yeshua waited to see what was about to happen.

As they broke through the roof, debris rained down on the floor in front of Yeshua, but he just leant back against the wall and watched in faint amusement. The hole they were digging got larger and larger.

The next thing that happened was that a bedraggled looking man who was clearly incapacitated, was hauled up onto the roof from the street outside, clinging to a stretcher which had ropes attached to each corner. They dragged him across the roof and proceeded to lower him down through the hole they had dug, right in front of Yeshua.

Nothing was said. The man looked terrified as he lay there unable to move, surrounded by senior men of the Jewish faith, all staring at him. He looked extremely uncomfortable and peered up at the four faces above him, looking for guidance. It would have been quite comical, but everyone was watching to see what Yeshua would do next.

Yeshua simply crouched down and calmly told the man that his sins were forgiven! It was as if he had just poked a wasp's nest with a stick.

Simon was busily writing everything down against an angry hum of indignation. What did he think he was saying? Only G_d could forgive sins. This was sheer blasphemy! Why was this man speaking this way?

Yeshua stood up slowly and faced the audience.

'Which is easier,' he questioned, 'to tell this man, "Your sins are forgiven" or simply to say to him, "Get up and walk"?'

This was a bit like throwing a large lump of fat into the fire. People at the back were getting up and just about to leave.

Yeshua took a step forward and, standing in front of the man, he looked round at the assembled leadership of the Jewish faith.

'Before you leave there is something you should know. The Son of Man does actually have authority on earth to forgive sins.' And with that he turned to the crippled man and ordered him to get up, go home and take his bed with him.

The man, who was well known in the town as The Paralysed Beggar, had his eyes fixed on Yeshua. He drew one leg up at first and with difficulty began to sit up. He moved his weight forward slowly and somewhat unsteadily, and then he struggled to his feet, standing precariously in front of Yeshua.

He bent forward still looking at Yeshua and picked up his mattress, ropes and all, and wobbled his way towards the door, looking for all the world as if he was sleep walking.

The look of astonishment spread across the faces of those present. For some their objections quickly turned to praise, but for others their misgivings were deepened. Meanwhile, the men on the roof had scrambled back down into the street, exclaiming their praises to G_d just as the healed man emerged into the daylight outside. Everyone was crying out and hugging one another in excitement until the noise from outside became quite deafening.

The Pharisee sitting next to Simon turned to his friend and shouted above the din. 'We have never seen anything like this!'

Simon made a note of it at the bottom of his wax pad.

Chapter 5

# JUDAS THE DISCIPLE

The noise slowly subsided as the guests drifted away. Peter's mother-in-law emerged into the courtyard and inspected the gaping hole in her roof. Then, with the help of some of the other women who followed Yeshua, they set about clearing up the mess.

Simon was chatting to an old friend, an official at the synagogue in Magdala, a town on the edge of the sea of Galilee just north of Tiberias. He broke off to speak to one of the women who was helping with the clearing up. Simon enquired as to who she was.

'She is Mary from Magdala,' he responded. 'She plays a key part in supporting Yeshua I'm told. She is very well connected, you know, and also a key benefactor of the synagogue, out of her own means I should add.' He smiled at Mary who was going back inside.

'Ah yes, I remember her, now you mention it. I thought I had come across her before. She used to support John the Baptist I recall. So how did she get involved with Yeshua?'

'I gather she was healed by him, or so the local story goes. She had been plagued by her past and there is even talk that she was demonised by these occurrences. Anyway, Yeshua delivered her from her condition, and she has followed him ever since.'

'So Yeshua has some solid backing financially?' asked Simon casually.

His friend looked at him quizzically. 'I suppose so,' he replied, 'You would be better talking to your nephew, Judas; he holds the purse strings. It's been nice catching up with you, Simon. I need to be going. I should make it back to Magdala before nightfall.' And with that he departed.

Simon bid him goodbye and looked round for Judas, but he was nowhere to be seen. Then he spotted him across the courtyard talking with another man. Judas was surprised to see his old uncle.

'Uncle Simon! What are you doing here? I haven't seen you since we were with John the Baptist ages ago!' He embraced his much-loved uncle with a kiss and a hug.

'I'm just down from Jerusalem. I have some business in the area to attend to and I'm staying at the inn by the synagogue. How are you, anyway? Are you involved with Yeshua?'

'Yes I am. He has chosen me as one of his disciples.'

'Really? I thought you were still with John's disciples?' Simon asked, pretending not to know too much.

'I was, but when Yeshua presented himself for baptism John told us straight away that although he had been baptising us in water, Yeshua would baptise us in the Holy Spirit and fire! He virtually told us he was the Messiah, the Anointed one that the prophets talked about all those years ago,' Judas looked around to make sure no one else was listening, but his enthusiasm was infectious, 'so, I decided to follow him!' He lowered his voice. 'If he is going to redeem Israel,' he whispered, 'I want to be a part of it!'

'Do you think he will drive out the Romans?' enquired Simon discreetly.

Judas looked down. 'I'm not sure exactly. Sometimes I think he will, and then he says something which changes my mind. We will have to wait and see.' Judas looked up again. 'His demonstrations of power are something that only G_d could do, so maybe he will. It's too early to tell.'

'Quite so,' replied Simon nonchalantly. 'So will you invite me to join you while I'm here?' he asked. 'I have some spare time on my hands and should like to get to know a bit more about it all.' He smiled at Judas.

'Of course, Uncle Simon. I just need to find out where Yeshua is. He has a habit of just slipping away unnoticed. But we usually find him somewhere.' Judas looked around for some of the other Disciples. Then he spotted Simon the Fisherman, only he introduced him as Peter. The old scribe was somewhat confused. They chatted for a few moments and then Peter turned to leave.

'That was Simon the Fisherman…right?' Simon asked.

'Yes, but Yeshua calls him Peter. He gave him a new name when he called him to be a follower. He gives quite a few of us nicknames like that.'

'Ah, I see.' said Simon, none the wiser.

Judas continued. 'Yeshua has this way of seeing things from a totally different perspective. He calls it the Kingdom of G_d. Take Peter for example. When you get to know Peter the "Rock", you might be forgiven for thinking "What Rock?" He's quite the opposite! But Yeshua sees things in people that no one else knows are there.'

Judas and Simon went through into the main part of the house, and they sat down alone together at a small table in the corner of the room.

'This Kingdom he refers to,' asked Simon, 'could that be something which is totally different in reality?'

'What do you mean?' asked Judas.

'Well, I was wondering, listening to him earlier, whether he might have another purpose. Perhaps his Kingdom is rooted in the Scriptures. David writing in the Psalms talks about an everlasting Kingdom. And then in the first book of Chronicles David also refers to the Kingdom lasting forever but here he states that he, David, will be ruler forever and then he explains that this Kingdom is rooted in his ancestor Judah. In other words, the Kingdom is always there even if on earth there is no King on the throne. So you could say it's a Kingdom of Heaven or of G_d.'

'Wow, Uncle Simon. I am always amazed at your knowledge of the Scriptures! How do you do it?'

Simon smiled in a kindly way as Judas studied his favourite uncle with affection.

'Years and years of copying the Scriptures onto new scrolls for synagogues around the region, Judas, and when I write I speak out every word as I do it. That way you don't make a mistake, but the other benefit is that you tend to remember it also.' He went on. 'David was not just a king in the spiritual sense you know, he was actually a king in the real world.' He paused to study Judas. 'Do you think Yeshua is the promised Messiah who will re-establish the Kingdom of Israel?'

Judas looked back into Simon's eyes. He had grown up in the shadow of his uncle. Someone he had always looked up to. Could he trust Simon? One thing growing up had taught him was that you can't be too careful in this world. That was the question going through his mind. He wasn't quite sure.

'You've seen what he did today, Uncle Simon. What do you think?' he replied, playing safe.

'Oh, it's far too early for me to say.' Simon replied before venturing to put the question in a different way. 'But you have been with him quite a while. You've heard him teach, watched him cast out demons, heal the sick people and you've had the opportunity to sit at his feet in private. Does he not talk about re-taking the throne of Israel? Does he not mention the Messiah, the one anointed to sit on the throne of Israel?'

Judas felt a bit uncomfortable and a bit cautious. 'He does talk a lot about the Kingdom of G_d and quite often the demons cry out that they know who he is; that he is the Son of G_d, but then he tells them to shut up and when he heals someone, he often tells them not to tell anyone about it.

'Are you saying, Uncle Simon, that the real Messiah will establish a Kingdom like the Kingdom of David,' he lowered his voice 'something that will overthrow the Romans and liberate Israel to be free once again?'

As Judas spoke, he glanced around to see if he was being watched. He knew the room was empty, but it was an automatic reaction. You couldn't be too careful; these were dangerous times.

Simon leaned in towards him as if to say something important and confidential. 'Well, that's what the Scripture says.' He leant back and, sensing enough had been said for now, changed the subject. 'Come on. Let's see if we can catch up with Yeshua.'

The other disciples had already left. Peter's mother-in-law was by the door on the other side of the room, hands on hips.

She was surveying the dust all over the room from dozens of feet tramping through her house.

'Tut! Tut!' she muttered, 'It's going to take me the rest of the day to clear up this mess to be sure.'

Chapter 6

# TEACHING BY THE SEA

Out in the street it was not difficult to see where the crowd had got to. You only had to look for the cloud of dust drifting up the hillside in the afternoon breeze. They hurried along the coastal path until they caught up.

They found Yeshua and the other disciples by the water's edge around a small bay. Yeshua was in a fishing boat a short distance from the shore and was standing in the boat speaking to the crowd. The crowd were spread out around the bay with some at the water's edge and those behind on the slightly higher ground leading down to the shore. The sea breeze carried his voice across the water towards the crowd so that all could hear clearly.

Simon and Judas soon found a place where they could sit and hear every word. Simon got out his wax tablets and stylus and settled down to listen. At first, he had difficulty engaging with what was being said. It sounded like a series of stories about everyday life, and he couldn't quite grasp the meaning of where his teaching was going. It was clear that the crowd were hanging on every word. It was quite unlike anything he had ever heard before.

Then Yeshua stopped speaking and raised his hand. The crowd fell silent. All you could hear was the rustling of reeds around the water's edge. The sea lapped against the dark volcanic stones along the shoreline. A little girl just next to him had her hood up to protect against the sun and the edge of it flapped gently in the breeze. A small colourful bird swooped down, twittering as it went, and perched on a nearby branch. It was suddenly all very peaceful.

Yeshua put his hand behind his ear. 'Listen!' he said.

Everyone strained to hear, but there was so much to hear. What should they be listening for? People looked about them, not sure what they should focus on.

Then, shading his brow from the sun with one hand, with the other he pointed up the slope to a rough patch of ground in the distance. The crowd turned to look. In the distance you could just make out a farmer with a heavy shoulder bag of seed broadcasting it this way and that, walking to and fro across his field.

Everyone strained to see. It was a pretty rubbishy sort of field either side of a small path. Some of it looked worth farming but the rest was either briars or rocks. It looked as if it needed a good sorting out.

As the crowd watched, the farmer swung his arm and seed scattered over the entire field, lying on the surface before he could plough it in. From behind, brown necked ravens and collared doves stole what seed they could from the paths and exposed places before he could return. The crowd watched for some time in the shimmering heat of the afternoon sunshine.

Simon wondered what the point of all this was.

'What did you see?' asked Yeshua as the crowd returned their attention to him.

'The sower went out to sow!'

'Did you notice that when he sowed, some seed fell on the path? And then the birds swooped down and pecked it up? Did you see that?'

The crowd listened intently. Many were farmers and knew exactly what he was talking about.

'And then some of the seed fell on stony patches, and you know what will happen to that when it springs up?'

The crowd chuckled attentively.

'With not much soil, the sun will scorch it, and it won't stand a chance without any root structure. And then, you see, some seed will end up among the briars, and when the plough goes in they will both get buried, but the brambles will take over and choke off the crop.

'But you saw some of the seed falling onto decent ground and that's where most of the harvest will come from. And you know what? That seed will yield maybe thirty times what is planted, perhaps even sixty times. And if you can believe it, some may

even produce a yield a hundred times as much as what was sowed.'
Some of the farmers there looked incredulous.

He paused for a second.

'If you have the sort of ears that can hear what I can hear,
then you will know what I am saying.' Yeshua looked around
the crowd expectantly.

Simon was a bit mystified. Clearly, he didn't have the right
sort of ears, because it made absolutely no sense to him. He had
heard John the Baptist speak. He spoke with power and conviction, but what was all this about? Perhaps it had some sort of cod-
ed meaning which would become clear later? So he wrote it all
down and hoped for the best.

'What did you make of all that, Judas?'

Judas shook his head. 'I don't really know.' He confessed.
'He often speaks about the Kingdom of G_d like this, in sort of
riddles, like Samson, and he often just uses the things that are
all around us – everyday things which we would ignore otherwise.' Judas slowly shook his head again and raised his eyebrows.

Later that evening there was an opportunity to get together
with the key twelve disciples and some close followers which he
had chosen to be with him. Everyone was keen to get the inside
story as to what these illustrations actually meant.

They had returned to Peter's house and were gathered around
a small metal brazier in the outside courtyard behind the house.
The hole in the roof was still evident, diverting smoke through
the opening.

'To you, the mystery of the Kingdom of G_d has been giv-
en,' began Yeshua as the last disciples were settling themselves
down on the cushions scattered around the floor. Simon started
to write down his words, and as he wrote the words "Kingdom of
G_d" he thought to himself that this was what he wanted to hear.

'But to those outside they get everything in parable stories.

'Because while seeing they may see and yet not know what
they are looking at and while hearing they won't understand,
otherwise they would turn back and be forgiven.'

The disciples didn't really understand what Yeshua was saying, but Simon recognised that he was quoting from a passage from the prophet Isaiah!

Simon's ears pricked up as he wrote. He knew this passage well. It was Isaiah's Great Commission, to prophesy in a way that would only be understood in the last days, when Israel would be nothing more than a stump of the old tree.

Then he remembered that those people who had returned from exile in Babylon who saw themselves as the offspring of David had settled in Nazareth. They saw themselves as the tender green shoot from the old stump, the descendants of the ancient Davidic line; in Hebrew, the Netzer (green shoot). These were Netzarenes settling in Netzareth, now known as Nazarenes from Nazareth, and this is where Yeshua came from!

Suddenly the penny dropped. It made Yeshua much more of a political Messiah than it would appear on the surface. 'Perhaps that old rogue Caiaphas knew more than he was letting on,' he thought. 'Perhaps he was right to be concerned.'

Was Yeshua's mission intended to be 'hidden'? Was the real meaning behind the stories he was telling intended principally for the ears of the followers he was training? Was this 'Kingdom' he kept referring to in reality a political Kingdom?

The temptation was to ask too many questions when he was in a privileged position to do so, but that would jeopardise his cover too soon. Instead, he would listen and take notes.

All that evening Yeshua was explaining his riddles, his parables, to his disciples. Always it came down to an explanation of his so called 'Kingdom of G_d'.

Simon carefully wrote down all that he was saying, being careful to record the exact words so that he could study them carefully later and refer back to the scriptures for clues.

The thing that niggled him was that the parables on their own would actually be insufficient to bring about a satisfactory conviction. What he needed was something more controversial; something which was blasphemous or broke the law in some way.

Forgiving a man's sins was an act that only G_d could do. For anyone else to do that was blasphemous, but on the other hand, whatever sin had caused the paralysis of the man who was healed that morning had clearly been forgiven, since the outcome was that he was healed. It was hard to argue with that, but the very personal way he conducted the affair raised a degree of doubt. He had clearly and openly said 'Which is easier? To say to this paralytic, "Your sins are forgiven," or to say, "Get up and walk!"'

If nothing had occurred things would be different, but the outcome was undoubtedly a stumbling block.

It was getting late. Simon decided to call it a day. He bade goodnight to Judas and slipped out, returning to the inn by the synagogue.

As he lay back on his bed turning over the events of the day in his mind, he realised he needed to try and break the code of the parables and unlock the true purpose of Yeshua's mission.

The next day he awoke early. He hadn't slept too well, so he got up and went straight down to Fisherman's Lane. Even so, there was a large crowd gathering in the half light. Many were sick and seeking healing.

Simon had a hard time getting through to the door. Finally, with his hand covering his nose and mouth, he managed to get in. Some of the close disciples were not there, and soon it became clear that Yeshua was missing. He had got up before anyone else and had slipped out unnoticed. How he had got past the waiting crowd unrecognised, some of whom had been there all night, was a mystery, but apparently it had happened before.

Had he sussed out Simon's mission and fled? And where was Judas? He was missing as well.

While Simon waited, he helped himself to some rather stale bread and water in preparation for the day.

After about an hour there was still no sign of him, and then Judas returned. He had been out buying some provisions for the group.

'Where do you think Yeshua has gone?' Simon asked.

'Oh, he often does this. Sometimes he disappears for hours.'

Judas unloaded some of the provisions from a large basket.

'Peter and John have found the places where he likes to go to pray. I think he just finds people pressing in on him all the time very demanding and he likes to get away where he can be alone.'

'So he has not gone off to meet anyone else?'

Judas wondered what was behind Uncle Simon's question. 'No, why should he?'

Simon just shrugged his shoulders and turned to help him unload the supplies.

'He likes to be apart so that he can listen to what his Father is telling him. It's an important part of how he operates. He encourages us to listen too, but personally I don't really understand what he means.

'Recently we spent the whole evening practising listening. I'm afraid I just fell asleep, but I wasn't alone! I didn't 'hear' or 'see' anything unfortunately.'

'What do you mean "hear or see"?' enquired Simon.

'Yeshua seems to be constantly 'seeing' what he refers to as "what the Father is doing." As far as I can see it's like a sort of premonition of what's going to happen. So, when events unfold that he has previously 'seen' happening, he knows that it is what his Father wants him to do. He has some extraordinary insights sometimes, particularly into people's lives. It can be quite unnerving at times.

'He's always encouraging us to do the same, but it doesn't really happen for me.' Judas stopped and stared at the floor, looking quite dejected. 'I sometimes wish I could 'see and hear' like some of the others.' He paused to fold up the baskets. 'I'm not alone, of course,' he went on, 'some of the others struggle a bit too.'

Judas scooped up the baskets and disappeared into the little storage cupboard off the kitchen area. When he returned his spirits had lifted.

'Uncle Simon, if you'll excuse me, I have quite a bit to do. We were due to leave shortly, and I expect Peter and John will have found Yeshua by now, so we need to get ready to leave for wherever he's going to take us today.'

'So you don't know where you're going today?' Simon seemed a bit puzzled that there was no clear plan of action.

'Oh, we never know where we're going. It's quite exciting really. Never a dull moment!' Judas went out to collect some more supplies leaving Simon to fend for himself.

Simon stood there, reflecting on what Judas had been saying, when suddenly the door burst open and in walked Peter and John, and in between them was Yeshua. He passed right by Simon, and as he did so their eyes met. His presence in the room changed the whole atmosphere, it was extraordinary, and his eyes...his eyes seemed not to look *at* Simon; rather they seemed to look right *into* him. It was a most unsettling sensation. The three of them went straight through into the courtyard.

Simon waited inside, feeling rather awkward. Then Judas returned with an armful of bread. No one said anything. The crowd outside was getting noisier, with some people crying out, having seen Yeshua return.

The sun was rising, and light was streaming in through the gap between the lean-to roofs and through the open door to the courtyard.

Then, in a moment of extraordinary serenity, Yeshua appeared in the doorway. He wasn't in any way hurried, and as the sunlight silhouetted his frame the whole room seemed to fill with light reflected off his white tunic. Simon felt himself being enveloped in a deep sense of peace.

Yeshua was quite a big man, but there was a gentleness to him which was particularly noticeable when he moved. His movements were not hurried in any way. It gave him a strong presence of calm and authority. Simon had heard people speaking about this, but now he could see it for himself.

Yeshua looked at Simon once again, only this time Simon felt quite different. He felt an unusual sense of friendliness, a sense of love, and then he smiled at Simon. Yeshua had not spoken directly to Simon before, but he sensed that things were about to change.

'You're Simon, Judas' relative, aren't you?' he asked.

'Yes, I'm his uncle,' he replied.

Immediately he felt guilty because he knew it wasn't the truth. The magical moment was broken. Then he felt a rising sense of fear. Was Yeshua going to expose him? It was like having your soul laid bare. He could feel Yeshua looking at him in that exposing, uncomfortable way.

'Uncle?' asked Yeshua. Simon's heart nearly stopped. 'A truly special relationship, no doubt.' Yeshua looked at Simon and smiled. Simon was not a big man anyway. If he was small, he now felt even smaller.

'Yes, very special, Rabbi,' he replied respectfully. He could feel his vocal cords tightening as he spoke.

'Come with us, Simon, and be my guest. Then I will show you the Father.' He smiled at him again. 'In the Father you will know the truth, and the truth will set you free!'

'Thank you, Rabbi. I am most grateful to you.'

Simon could barely speak, and beads of perspiration were breaking out on his forehead. He felt utterly naked. Never before had he experienced anything quite like it.

Out in the street, in the full light of day, the crowd fell silent as Yeshua emerged from the house.

Peter and several of the disciples went ahead in front as usual, forming a cordon around Yeshua as they moved slowly, heading north towards the coastal road to Bethsaida.

Now and again people would manage to break through the cordon, pleading for mercy to be healed of their afflictions. Yeshua would stop and often he would heal them, sometimes dealing directly with the illness or addressing an underlying issue.

On one such occasion a man suffering from leprosy was standing by the side of the road. The crowd recoiled in revulsion. To everyone's amazement and horror, the man approached the front of the crowd. The disciples shrank back, but Yeshua stood still. It was a tense moment, and the man was desperate. He fell on his knees right in front of Yeshua pleading to be healed.

'If you are willing, you can cleanse me,' he asked in a near whisper as if daring himself to ask, his head bowed.

Yeshua looked at him as if indignant at his question. Then he stepped forward towards the man. Loud gasps could be heard as he put his hand *on* the man. Deep down there was a concern that the leper would defile Yeshua, and what then would happen to those he touched afterwards? Would they also be made unclean?

And then, in quite a matter-of-fact voice full of compassion, he said, 'Well of course I'm willing!' And, sensing how the man was feeling and how the crowd was thinking, he added, 'You *are* clean! Clean and not defiled!'

The man withdrew his arm from under his garment and looking at it, realised that it was no longer leprous. As he began to examine other parts of his body, he realised that he had been totally restored. He then felt his face as he got to his feet and stood there looking through his fingers, not daring to lower them in case it was all a dream. But as he lowered his hands the people around him could see that his face was perfectly clear, with great big tears tumbling down over his clear skin. He just stood there, sobbing uncontrollably.

Simon had been close enough to witness the whole thing. The man was horribly disfigured on his arm and face as he knelt in front of Yeshua. Now as he looked up at Yeshua it seemed to Simon and others that for all the world there had been some sort of mistake. The disfigurement that everyone thought they had seen before was no longer there. Had they imagined his leprosy?

Then Yeshua said something as he sent him away which Simon didn't quite understand. It was a strong warning and Simon wrote it down, as it struck him as correct but a bit of a contradiction. He told the man not to tell anyone about his healing encounter but to go and show himself to the priest, carefully following the ritual cleansing rules laid down by Moses.

Why should he keep it secret? It didn't make sense to Simon. However, it would very quickly become clear why.

News of his healing spread throughout the crowd and as people learned what had happened there were spontaneous shouts of praise to G_d.

As a result, their journey soon became impeded by ever more desperate people, pressing in on Yeshua so that progress became impossible.

Peter consulted with Yeshua, and the other disciples and it was decided to try and go back to an area where they had found Yeshua earlier. It was a fairly inhospitable piece of land in a slightly elevated position above the sea which was apparently deserted. The grass was long and unkempt, with rocks strewn around a sort of bowl. Nobody seemed to know who it belonged to.

When they arrived, it was getting hot, and so Yeshua had them sit down on the grass around the hillside while the disciples set up a cordon at the bottom of the hill, from behind which Yeshua could speak to the people.

He spoke for several hours using illustrations from the surroundings, depicting some image or other of the Kingdom of G_d.

He would use images of the wildflowers, the grass, and many well understood farming illustrations. Those who listened could easily identify with these images, living as they did in a world which revolved around nature.

It was as if he was going out of his way to distance himself from the religious authorities and their world of rules and regulations. The authorities had a way of making people feel subdued and very small and insignificant, but here was a man who was presenting the Kingdom of G_d with pictures of things which were insignificant; things like the smallest of all seeds, like the mustard seed, insignificant in size yet growing into something much more significant.

Simon's suspicions grew. He was certain that a political perspective was unfolding.

Then Yeshua began to teach that the people in this world who were clearly cursed by the hopelessness of their situations, people like the very poor, people who didn't have enough to stave off hunger, people who wept in their distress, downtrodden in every respect, people who found no justice in this world, who were constantly persecuted, all these people, the ones who the authorities and those who interpreted the law looked down on as accursed, these self-same people Yeshua saw as blessed and the people who mattered most in his Kingdom. Instead of making the people feel small he made them feel quite the opposite. They felt valued, important, affirmed, and they felt a sense of belonging. It was outrageous, thought Simon!

Yeshua spoke out against the rich, the well fed and those who held powerful positions in society. These were the people who everyone else saw as being the blessed. They had it all. But it got worse. His followers were being urged to love their enemies, would you believe?! The enemies of Israel to be loved? What utter rubbish!

The idea was ridiculous! Who could survive in a world where people loved their enemies? Was he really expecting them to love the Romans? It was verging on blasphemy to love the enemies of Israel!

He was telling these people that instead of being the accursed, which they had to admit was what it felt like under Roman and Jewish rule, that instead they were actually the blessed ones! It was like music to their ears.

Simon was convinced that this Yeshua man was trying to whip up the sympathy of the public, who he was clearly trying to groom for action against the authorities. Somehow, he must be stopped.

Yeshua's stinging comments against the Pharisees and Simon's fellow scribes were nothing less than an undisguised and direct attack which left him feeling outraged.

Simon busily took down as much material as he could. Later he would have to write up this material onto some scrolls. Right now, he was fast running out of wax tablets.

But central to his mission was to persuade Judas to corroborate all the evidence that he was gathering and to persuade him to bear witness to all that was being said. The tricky bit would be how to turn him sufficiently to facilitate an arrest.

Simon realised he needed a plan and one that would work.

That night he returned to Capernaum. In the morning he would ask the rabbi at the synagogue for a blank scroll on which to transcribe the evidence he had collected. He would also use the time to hatch a plan. Simon found hatching plans rather agreeable.

# Chapter 7

# A DEMON ENCOUNTER

That night, Yeshua, recognising the difficulty of travelling by road, took the entire party off by boat to get away from the crowds. They set sail in two fishing boats heading for the other side of the Sea of Galilee. Unfortunately, the weather closed in, and a powerful gale blew up.

According to a report from Judas after they returned, the boats were very nearly overwhelmed by the sudden east wind which whipped the sea into a frenzy. Apparently, Yeshua was asleep in the stern during all the chaos. It was rapidly getting dark, and they were out in deep water trying to bail out their sinking vessels. The boat carrying Yeshua, in which Judas was also travelling, was in danger of sinking.

They woke Yeshua up. He seemed unconcerned; in fact, he was actually quite annoyed and contemptuous of their predicament, as if the weather was just a crude attempt to stop them reaching their destination!

According to Judas, Yeshua stood up and actually shouted at the storm! He treated it as you would a disobedient dog!

'Get down!' he ordered, 'Be still!' and he held up his hand with all the confidence of a military commander.

Suddenly everything went quiet and calm, and the wind dropped. It was an extraordinary experience, quite frightening actually. One minute they were in the teeth of a gale with waves breaking over the boats and the next it stopped, and everything went eerily quiet. It was so unexpected. In all their experience of being on the sea they had never seen such a sudden change in the weather.

Then he turned to the disciples and soundly ticked them off for being scared and not having any faith. Judas couldn't swim and didn't like boats anyway, so felt somewhat aggrieved.

Before continuing their journey, they had to bail out the boats. Hardly anyone dared speak. They were pretty scared. 'Who is this man?' asked Thomas, one of the disciples, in a hushed whisper to Judas.

By daybreak they had reached the other side and were about to find out that it wasn't just nature at work trying to hinder Yeshua's crossing. There may have been a link to the forces ranged against him during the night; something much more powerful and sinister.

They had been blown way off course during the crossing by a strong easterly Sharkiyeh wind, which had driven the boats further south.

This was unfamiliar territory.

No sooner had they beached the boats on a barren stretch of shoreline than they were confronted by a terrifying sight.

With a scalp tingling scream a man sprang from behind some rocks and headed straight for the boats. He was completely naked, with long matted hair, and his body and arms were hunched forward in an aggressive manner. His eyes were staring out of his head and his whole face was contorted in an ugly grimace.

Those who had started up the beach spun around and beat a hasty retreat back to the boats. They were terrified.

All, that is, except Yeshua. He calmly walked towards the monstrous apparition. The man stopped a short distance away.

Yeshua challenged the unclean spirit to come out of the man.

This provoked an extraordinary reaction. He lunged forwards at a run, as if to attack Yeshua, but instead fell face down at his feet and, with a deafening howl of anguish, he shouted out at Yeshua not to torment 'them' and called him the Son of the Most High G_d.

Undeterred, Yeshua spoke directly to the demon to give up his name.

'Your name,' he demanded, 'give me your name!' He raised his voice impatiently, staring at the man almost aggressively.

'My name is Legion,' he grudgingly replied.

Immediately the man, who had been living among some graves nearby, and who they later learnt possessed superhuman strength, began pleading with Yeshua not to expel 'them' from the country.

In a bizarre twist to the story, the demons asked to be sent into the herd of domesticated boar that were foraging nearby in pasture on top of the cliffs. Perhaps this was a ploy to evade destruction, or perhaps these boars were being bred for demonic sacrifice.

Yeshua agreed, and no sooner had he consented than the boar spooked in a confusion that quickly escalated into a stampede. Their squeals echoed eerily over the cliff edge and down the hill.

Everyone watched in astonishment and fear as the stampede gathered pace, tails erect, but Yeshua watched with the hint of a smile as the herdsmen tried in vain to divert a disaster.

But there was nothing they could do as they bunched up against the cliff edge. And then they were gone, down the steep slope towards the sea. When they reached the bottom, they just kept going straight into the sea. Unaccustomed to water, they quickly drowned.

The delivered man lay there motionless at the feet of Yeshua, who bent down and, taking his hand, raised him to his feet. His face was no longer contorted, and his eyes were fixed on Yeshua.

The disciples found him some spare clothes, and when the herdsmen turned up with some of the local people in tow, they could hardly believe their eyes, seeing this madman now clothed and talking normally with Yeshua and the disciples.

The herdsmen were far from happy at the loss of their entire herd of boar. Soon they were demanding that the whole party depart and go home.

This liberated soul now wanted to come with them, but Yeshua told him to go back to his people and tell them what great things the Lord had done for him.

And so they bade him farewell and set sail back to Capernaum.

Chapter 8

# A PLAN DISCLOSED

It was getting late. Simon was finishing off writing up his notes in a back office of the Synagogue when Judas burst in.

'There you are, Uncle Simon; I've been looking everywhere for you. You simply won't believe what we have seen today!' He could hardly contain his excitement.

He began to relate all that had happened on the sea overnight and the extraordinary encounter they had witnessed in the deliverance of the man and his Legion demons.

'Slow down, Judas!' said Simon, searching for a fresh scroll to take down what was being related to him. 'Start again from the beginning.'

That day, Simon had transcribed nearly all the notes he had made on his wax tablets. The Rabbi had kindly offered to wipe them with a hot iron, ready for re-use. Most of his stock was ready to be wiped, which he would get done in the morning.

Now, stylus in hand, he began to note down Judas' account. When he had finished, he read back what he had written.

'You say the demonised man pleaded with Yeshua not to be sent out of the country?' he asked.

'Yes, he was quite emphatic about it,' replied Judas.

Simon rose from his bench and wandered over to the window, from where he could see the last of the sun setting on the heights above the Sea of Galilee, where all this drama had played out.

'You may not remember this account, Judas, but when the Israelites under Joshua's command first entered this area, they drove out a people called the Girgashites. They were known for practising the sacrifice of boar to demons. Joshua drove them right out of the country. Perhaps the demons were afraid Yeshua was going to do it all over again?"

'So you think they saw Yeshua as some sort of reincarnation of Joshua?' enquired Judas.

Simon thought for a minute. Could this be an opening to pursue his intention to turn Judas for his purposes?

'You say the demons called themselves "Legion"?' The old man scrutinised Judas. 'Do you think they had anything to do with the X Fretensis Roman Legion? The 10th Legion have a boar as their standard emblem, and since they are drawn from the local men of the area, who knows what practices they get up to?' he paused for a moment. 'How do you think he has control over these demons, Judas?'

'I honestly don't know. It must be part of his power and authority as Messiah. Maybe a demonstration of what is to come when he comes into his Kingdom,' replied Judas.

'Messiah, eh?' Simon raised his eyebrows and lowered his voice as he glanced over at the door to check it was closed. 'Do you see him as someone who will deliver Israel from her enemies?'

'If that happens, I don't fully understand how it will happen. One minute he is talking about a kingdom within the soul, and the next I wonder if this inner kingdom is going to be revealed by a deliverance of the whole nation of Israel. It's as if the possession of individuals and their deliverance is a foretaste of what he is going to do on a much bigger scale for the nation.'

'Do you think Yeshua was seen by the "Legion" as a direct threat to Roman rule at a spiritual level?' Simon ventured to make the connection between the deliverance that day and its possible political implications. He then saw an opportunity to sow a seed in Judas' mind that would have the potential for growth into a plan for his own objectives. He paused for a second or two to rehearse his thoughts before going on. 'You see, it's interesting you should mention the role of Messiah. One of the reasons I am here is to see how the authorities in Jerusalem might help bring this about. But you have to realise this is not for open discussion with anyone. You must swear to me that you will not discuss this with anyone, not even Yeshua at this stage.'

Judas looked at him with incredulity. 'Do you mean the authorities would be working behind the scenes to help Yeshua establish his Kingdom in the land?'

Simon wanted an answer to his question before he dared go any further. He put the question again. 'You must bind yourself to absolute secrecy, Judas. Do you swear?'

Judas paused to think. He had his suspicions, but his curiosity was unbearable.

'Yes, I swear myself by heaven to secrecy', he confessed.

'Good!' said Simon. 'Good man!' he repeated. 'If the Romans were to get wind of this, we'd all end up on a cross. You must realise the importance of what I am about to tell you.'

Simon took a deep breath, quickly evaluating in his scheming mind how he would tie Judas into his plan.

'The Romans are keen to make sure unrest is prevented at all costs. They know how these things can get out of hand. They like to be able to report to Rome that law and order are being well maintained, so any hint of dissent is stamped on hard.

'Don't be fooled. They might appear friendly sometimes, but they are not. They are here to govern and any challenge to their authority is taken very seriously.'

Simon was aware that Judas already knew all of this, but he was buying time to think.

'You see Judas, Caiaphas can't be seen to support insurrection, it would jeopardise the whole relationship between Rome and Jerusalem. It would put the very Temple at risk. Heaven forbid!

'However, if Yeshua were seen...' he paused, looking intently at Judas, '... if he were seen to be taken captive; as if he were being arrested; then he could be taken to the Temple, where he could work a miracle of power and overthrow the Romans with a word of his authority.' Simon was now pacing around the room, his hands gesticulating in the air. 'Don't you see, Judas? Once he has proclaimed himself King, and of course he is from the line of David, he could come into his Kingdom of power and take his rightful place on the throne of Israel!'

Simon's eyes were wide with enthusiasm, but Judas didn't look convinced.

'Why can't he do that from here?' he asked. 'Why would he need to go through all that rigmarole to proclaim himself King? It doesn't make sense.'

Simon's mind went into overdrive. He couldn't afford to see his plan fail. Then it came to him. He cleared his throat and his voice changed. He began to speak calmly in a matter-of-fact way.

'Just like David and all the kings of Israel, he needs to be anointed with oil by the High Priest – to be crowned King in Jerusalem; in the Temple, where all power and authority comes from Jehovah. The same power he has given to his people to rule and govern themselves, and he will never take that away.

'It's part of his Holy Covenant with his people – to rule through them. Yeshua knows this, and he will wait for the anointing to happen, and when it does his power will be made complete!

'Don't you see Judas? And you and I are the very key to how that will happen. Do you understand?'

As he was speaking he surprised himself. 'Where did that come from? Pure genius!' he thought to himself.

Judas looked at him, not knowing what to think. The Jewish authorities seemed very hostile towards Yeshua. Could this be the way, or was it simply a trap? He said nothing, but Simon could see what he was thinking.

'It's been a long day,' said Simon, changing his tone again. 'You must be very tired, and you need to rest. Don't forget, not a word to anyone. We will watch and pray together as we see the ministry of Yeshua unfold. It will all become clear. You'll see. You can trust your old uncle. You know that, don't you?' He gave Judas a big hug and a pat on the back. 'Now get some rest and we'll talk about it again soon.'

With that, they embraced again and Judas left, making his way down to Peter's mother-in-law's house in Fisherman's Lane to join Yeshua and the other disciples. His mind was awhirl.

Once inside the house he went to the cupboard and helped himself to some bread. He was hungry. He slumped down on a cushion and leant against the wall, trying to make sense of the past twenty-four hours. On the face of it, Uncle Simon's comments had a ring of truth to them, but on the other hand there was something not quite right about it. It niggled him. Above all he wanted to do the right thing. But the thought that he might be the person who would go down in history as the one who enabled Yeshua to deliver his people from the Romans, now that was quite an exciting thought!

It occurred to him that the events he had witnessed the night before, when even the wind and the sea obeyed Yeshua's command, all seemed so amazing that perhaps the thought of him overthrowing the hated Romans might not be that implausible.

As for the requirement that Yeshua needed to be anointed with oil by the High Priest in order to become King in his Kingdom, now this was definitely not something he had considered before.

# Chapter 9

# ENCOUNTER WITH THE LAWYERS

As the days and weeks ran into months, Simon and Judas followed this extraordinary man around the countryside, the towns, and the villages.

They witnessed him healing the sick and preaching the Kingdom of G_d, always using his parable stories to illustrate his 'Kingdom' but careful never to make public claims about who he was. In fact, he seemed to go out of his way to distance himself from fame, telling those who were healed to keep it silent and not to broadcast what they had experienced. Of course, they didn't, and the crowds kept following him and pressing him for more. It was utterly exhausting and yet, despite pushing himself relentlessly, he still found time to be apart in prayer and quietness as often as he could.

They were to witness people being brought back to life, huge crowds being fed from just a few loaves and fish, and on more than one occasion too. He healed the sick, delivered those tortured by demons, and even empowered his disciples to do the same, sending them on ahead of him as he toured the land. It was heady stuff. He even walked on the surface of the Sea of Galilee on one occasion.

For Judas, as with the rest of the disciples, being present with him was like living in another world, totally removed from 'reality'. All the things that were impossible normally, simply happened as a matter of course, as if they were totally natural.

For Simon, following along, it was unnerving and yet frustrating.

Yeshua never claimed to be the Messiah, and the people who followed him never publicly spoke about it, although there was a sort of unspoken realisation that no one else could be doing these things and not be the Messiah. The only public declarations of who everybody thought he was came from the demons, and they were resoundingly silenced by him for saying so before being cast out of their tormented hosts.

But he never seemed to be moving towards the kind of deliverance which the prophets had spoken about. How could he possibly make the transition from his work as it was, to a King of the People and Deliverer of the Land? It was a puzzle. The people who followed him were not the sort who could take up a weapon and fight. So how did he propose to do it?

As for evidence against the man, there was no shortage of occasions when he spoke out against the Jewish authorities, and he often seemed to break the rules of the day.

Simon continued to note his words verbatim whenever he spoke out against the structure and authority of the Pharisees and leaders. He also made sure he accurately recorded the details whenever he performed a miracle on the Sabbath against the law.

As there were many occasions when visiting parties of other scribes and Pharisees were present, it was useful to know that in the event of presenting his evidence that there would be reliable witnesses to corroborate Simon's record.

Although Simon was careful to note any public declarations of where Yeshua appeared to be suggesting a teaching contrary to the law, he found the use of parables annoying and frustrating. Why didn't he say what he meant and come out with it? He felt increasingly convinced there was a secret code in these parables which he would eventually be able to unlock, and which could provide the vital evidence he was looking for.

He noted that John the Baptist, whom he had followed in similar circumstances, spoke plainly, without parables. He made no mention of a "Kingdom" as Yeshua did. Simon felt sure that eventually Yeshua would trip up and let the cat out of the bag. Perhaps a few leading questions would do the trick? But he didn't want to raise any suspicions, so he decided to make use of some of the many visiting Pharisees who came up from Jerusalem on occasions. He decided that when the time was right, he would prime one of them to ask a few tricky questions to flush Yeshua out.

Simon had noted that Yeshua was indifferent about adhering to the formal rules about washing hands ceremonially before eating. His disciples, more used to grabbing a bite on the job while working as fishermen, didn't bother, and Yeshua said nothing to correct them.

One day some Pharisees and scribes had joined in with the crowd. The atmosphere was quite tense.

Simon knew one of the scribes, so he approached him and began chatting to him. It was midday and the crowd were eating during a break. They were talking about how often Galileans didn't observe the formal washing rites. In most cases it was impractical to do so, as the facilities were not present.

Simon saw his chance. He pointed out that the small group sitting behind Yeshua who were eating some bread at the time were in fact some of his closest followers, his disciples.

'I don't imagine some of the Pharisees here today would be too happy about that if they knew who the men were,' he commented.

'No,' said his friend, 'I see what you mean. I might take the opportunity to have a quiet word, don't you think, Simon?'

'That's up to you, my friend.' Simon made an excuse to return to his duties.

He melted away into the crowd and settled down with his notebook at the ready.

He didn't have to wait long.

'Rabbi,' interrupted one of the Pharisees, 'Why do your disciples not wash according to the tradition of their elders, but eat bread with impure hands?'

There was a stunned silence.

Two of the disciples, who were actually eating at the time, lowered the bread they were eating into their laps and discreetly swallowed what was in their mouths. The question had made them feel somewhat uncomfortable, but their eyes were fixed on Yeshua.

Yeshua was not best pleased. He rose to his feet and slowly approached the group.

'Isaiah had it right about you bunch of actors when he prophesied that you honour G_d with your lips but your hearts are a million miles away; that you cancel out your worship of G_d by making rules and regulations that are entirely man made!

'You put G_d's commandments on the backburner while you concentrate on your own manmade traditions!'

The crowd erupted in applause. No one had ever spoken to the Pharisees like this before.

While the group huddled together to work out a response, Yeshua waded in deeper.

'You know, it's very convenient isn't it, to forget about the commandments of G_d while concentrating on your traditions?'

The Pharisees were completely on the back foot. 'What is he talking about?' they muttered to one another.

Yeshua stared long and hard at them. They stood there indignantly waiting for the next onslaught.

Yeshua lowered his voice and spoke calmly to them.

'Moses said,' he turned to face the crowd, pausing before raising his voice, 'Moses said, "Honour your father and mother," didn't he?' He turned back to the group and walked right up to them, standing in front of them. They began to look apprehensive.

'He also said, "He who speaks evil of father or mother let him be put to death."

'But you say...' he paused, moving sideways to stand immediately in front of the Pharisee who had asked the question, looking him straight in the eye. '... but you say,' he said calmly and quietly, 'if a son makes a formal declaration to his parents that his estate is destined as a gift to G_d, he is free to live off that estate for the rest of his life, but because it is given to G_d the son is absolved from looking after his parents in their old age! What kind of a rule is that, I ask? Your rule, which has been handed down from generation to generation, completely invalidates the word of G_d! Where is the honour towards his parents in that?

'What are his parents supposed to do in their old age? Go begging? How can that be right before G_d?

'And that's not the only thing you do like that.' He turned back to the crowd.

'Listen to me, all of you, and try to understand. There is nothing outside the body which when swallowed will make that person a sinner; spiritually dirty. It's what comes out of him that makes him a sinner; what he says and does.' He gave the Pharisee one last chance to respond, but he said nothing.

Yeshua turned to his disciples with a faint smile on his lips, raising an eyebrow as if to say, 'Carry on, my friends!'

Yeshua continued teaching until late afternoon. When he had finished, he gathered up his disciples and headed back to their lodgings with Peter.

Once inside, no one dared say anything. Inwardly they were both elated and unnerved by the earlier incident.

Finally, Peter broke the silence.

'We don't quite understand the bit about what we eat,' he asked.

Yeshua seemed quite despondent. 'Don't tell me you're as empty headed as they are!' he chided. 'Look, every time you eat something there is no way you are making yourself a sinner. It's natural to eat. It doesn't make your heart bad. What you are and think is not corrupted by the food you eat. What you eat ends up going down the drain!'

He made his familiar gesture for them to gather round, before continuing softly.

'No, the things that corrupt are the things that come out of people. Evil thoughts from deep inside their hearts. Things like plans to go revelling in orgies, to steal from others, to kill others, to make off with other people's wives. When you have cravings and secret pleasures, and want other people's lifestyles which you don't have, and work out how to trick them into giving over what you want. Scheming against each other, even devising plans to use witchcraft to get your own way; speaking and spreading lies about others and trying to beat them down with arrogant talk. It's all foolish action and talk; that's what is truly evil, and it starts deep down when we allow such thoughts.'

Peter could see the sense in what Yeshua was saying, but inwardly he felt very inadequate, because much of what he was saying was a bit too close to the bone for comfort. The same could probably be said for the rest of them, and notably Judas, who was weighing up his discussion with his uncle from the night before.

As for Simon, he had entered the house with a wider group of close followers and was sitting next to Judas, busily writing in his wax notebook. If he felt anything, it didn't show. He was perched on a small cushion. A dim glow from an oil lamp flickered on a stand next to him, bathing the two of them in a soft light.

John, one of Yeshua's closest disciples, was watching them. Their two profiles were side by side. Apart from a few more lines on Simon's face, the two men looked identical – more like father and son than uncle and nephew he thought. The family likeness was remarkable.

Yeshua began to elaborate on what he had been saying, and the disciples probed his teaching with questions and discussions late into the evening.

One of them, having seen how he dealt with the Pharisees earlier in the day, wanted to know if this new teaching was a replacement for the Law and the writings of the Prophets.

Yeshua seemed quite taken aback. 'Don't think for one minute that I have come to do away with the Law and the Prophets. Far from it! I've come to fulfil all that is written. No, that would be a complete misunderstanding! While creation exists not a single letter will disappear from the original Law. Not until everything written has been accomplished.

'You see, anyone who tries to omit the very least of what is written will find themselves treated as very least in the Kingdom of G_d, but those who keep and teach the scriptures will be Number One.

'Make a note of what I am saying, that you need to do better than the Pharisees and the teachers of the Law or you have no place in the Kingdom.'

Yeshua paused until Simon had finished writing, looking straight at him. Soon all eyes were on Simon. Glancing up on account of the silence, Simon became acutely aware of his predicament. He was making a note alright, but not exactly living up to the spirit of what Yeshua was suggesting.

Yeshua turned his attention back to the gathering. 'You see,' he said and then glancing back at Simon he added, 'Every teacher of the Law who has become a follower of the Kingdom of G_d is like the head of a family who collects modern silverware and yet has no difficulty in displaying it alongside the family heirlooms.'

He smiled at Simon and then continued his teaching.

Simon had run out of wax notepads and was frantically looking through his pockets. His fingers alighted on a single pad which had become detached, and he quickly jotted down the gist of what Yeshua had just said to him. He had been momentarily distracted and he hadn't fully taken in what Yeshua had been saying. Was he including him, Simon, who was a teacher of the Law, among his disciples, a follower of the Kingdom of G_d? Did he not know his true purpose? 'Maybe not,' he thought, which made him feel emboldened by the experience.

Then he remembered he had a spare book of tablets in his shoulder bag, which he quickly retrieved.

Yeshua went on with his teaching about people's personal conduct. His knowledge of the scriptures was impressive, and he often quoted from them.

His teaching was very radical. He seemed to see old truths in a very different light.

Another long day had come to an end, and every day was different.

Simon could feel himself being drawn in, but he also felt a strong feeling of caution, like a bird hopping tentatively forwards into a baited net trap in search of food. His motive was changing. At first, he had felt a sense of compulsion; his arm twisted by the High Priest; his reputation at stake. Now he felt a creeping curiosity. What he was witnessing was surreal and extraordinary, but at the same time it happened so often, miracle after miracle, acts of power unlike anything he had seen or even heard of before, that it became commonplace, a part of ordinary everyday life.

The puzzling thing was that, as a person, Yeshua was anything but extraordinary. He was in some respects ordinary; the sort of person you felt you could get to know. But at the same time there was an unsettling presence in his company. It was partly because he had this unnerving way of making one feel utterly exposed. There was nothing hidden from him, no secrets, no inner thoughts. He often seemed to know what people were thinking before they had even opened their mouths.

The longer Simon spent collecting his evidence, the more he felt confused about his mission, about his motives and about Yeshua, and even about his whole purpose in life.

He went to bed with his mind in a whirl, but fortunately he was a sound sleeper and awoke the next day untroubled by the doubts of the night before. He just pulled himself together and got on with the day.

By contrast, the mood amongst the group the following morning was decidedly nervous. They had received news that Herod Antipas was seeking to entice Yeshua to come and perform a miracle for him.

Yeshua himself was nowhere to be seen, but the disciples were hopeful he had spent the early hours of the morning in his customary place in a small cave on the nearby hillside.

Peter and John went off in search of him. Yeshua was not surprised to hear the news, but he wasn't about to fall for such an obvious trap.

He sat quietly in the early morning light at the entrance of the cave, looking out across the Sea of Galilee. He sat very still. The two disciples began to feel an extraordinary sense of peace come over them. But Yeshua's thoughts had moved on.

'The people of Tyre and Sidon need to hear about the Kingdom,' he said, breaking the silence, and rising to his feet he headed off down the hill. An hour later they were on the road again, headed northwest.

Meanwhile, Simon had decided to write up his notes and stayed behind. He was due to report back to Caiaphas, so he took the time to prepare a report for him, which he dispatched that day.

Reading through the material he had written up, he realised that although Yeshua sailed pretty close to the wind, he hadn't actually made any direct claims to be the Messiah, and his use of parables was a clever way of putting some distance between himself and what he was saying. Despite the circumstantial evidence mounting against him, there was no denying the sheer weight of miraculous signs being performed daily which could only be from G_d himself. Yeshua's miracles and healings were an acute embarrassment to Simon's case.

Chapter 10

# FIRST REPORT

The duty officer was at his desk in the Guard Room of the High Priest's Palace in Jerusalem when the post arrived.

Among the routine mail a small scroll was marked '*Private and Confidential. For the personal attention of the High Priest only.*'

'Guard!' barked the duty officer summoning the young man outside his door. 'Take this scroll immediately to the High Priest and deliver it to him personally. If you are unable to deliver it personally, you are to bring it straight back here. Do you understand?'

'Yes, sir!' The guard took the scroll and set off at his customary trot down the path towards the Palace entrance.

Once inside he made his way to the office of the High Priest and explained his purpose to the doorkeeper.

'The High Priest is busy. Give me the document and I'll see that he gets it later.'

'My orders are to deliver it to him personally or return it to the Guard Room,' he replied.

Realising the sensitivity of the situation, the doorkeeper turned and knocked on the door.

'Come!' ordered Caiaphas, and when the door was opened the guard could see the High Priest sitting behind a mound of scrolls at his desk. He did not look best pleased.

'What do you want?' he asked testily.

'I have a communication, Your Holiness, which is marked Private and Confidential, and the Guard is instructed to hand it to you personally.' The guard stood waiting to approach.

'Very well, let's be having it boy.' The High Priest stood up and beckoned the guard to come forward. Taking the scroll, he dismissed the two of them and eagerly broke open the seal.

He sat on the edge of the desk in front of an open window looking out across Jerusalem. He quickly read through the report from Simon. He was annoyed at the lack of progress.

He thought for a moment.

He picked up a small bell from his desk and rang it vigorously to summon his secretary.

He would call a meeting of the twenty-three-man Sanhedrin Council of the Court of the High Priest. Some of them had been up in the Galilee and had first-hand experience of this man Yeshua. He wanted action now.

The secretary took down some details and quickly left to arrange a meeting of the Council for the following day.

When they met no one but the High Priest had any idea what the 'Emergency Meeting' was all about. As they filed into the Council Chamber, one by one, there was a buzz of discussion among the members.

The Council Clerk banged his staff noisily on the flagstone floor and called the members to order. Taking their seats, they awaited the entry of the High Priest.

Two tall doors at the opposite end of the Chamber swung open and the secretary swept in, followed by the High Priest flanked by his two guards. Meanwhile the clerk bid the members rise.

Taking his seat at the head of the oval chamber, the members stood at their seats on either side, in two semicircles facing each other across the large stone flagged debating floor.

Overhead was an elaborate circular chandelier fitted with oil lamps facing outwards. High shuttered windows surrounded the chamber, through which sunlight pierced the gloom and bathed the white floor in strips of coloured light.

The plain whitewashed walls reflected the light into every corner of this very simple hall. The only decoration was a row of seven battered shields which hung on the wall behind the throne of the High Priest. It was believed that they once belonged to King David's fighting men. Each one carried the scars of hand-to-hand engagement with the King's enemies. Some held that they had once been among a thousand shields that hung on David's

Tower, but these were the only ones that had survived the turbulent history of the Jewish nation.

'The Council may be seated,' announced the clerk. His words echoed around the cedar-beamed ceiling. The rustle of the members taking their seats died back.

After the customary prayers, the High Priest Caiaphas rose to his feet, stepping down into the debating forum. He paced around in front of the assembly, glowering at the Members of Council while gathering his thoughts.

'Let me get straight to the point,' he began in his usual fashion, predictable and repetitive, blunt and brief. 'I've brought you here to discuss a matter of national security. A man who goes by the name of Yeshua from Nazareth poses a significant threat to our nation and all that we stand for. He may be plotting a political takeover. Some of you here may have personal experience of his arrogance and his methods.

'It is my judgement that he should be stopped and the sooner the better.'

There was ripple of disquiet from the gathering. A man named Nicodemus rose to his feet.

'May I ask, Your Holiness, what this man has done to offend us so?' He was one of the Pharisees who had personal experience of Yeshua's ministry.

Caiaphas was in no mood to be challenged. 'Are you one of his disciples too?' he asked. 'Has it passed you by, my learned friend, that to lay claim to be the Messiah is blasphemy deserving the death penalty?

Nicodemus responded. 'I have experience of listening to this man speak, and I have not actually heard him make such a claim. The many people who follow him may have their own personal views, but I have not heard him make such a claim in person, Your Holiness.

'As the Passover Festival is approaching and it is customary for people to come to Jerusalem to make their sacrifices to G_d, may I suggest that when he and his disciples come that it would be a good opportunity to question him face to face?'

There were murmurs of approval from the assembly.

Others in the chamber also voiced their concerns, and after a fairly heated debate it was decided to confront Yeshua at the earliest opportunity, and one or two were appointed to take charge of questioning.

This was not what Caiaphas wanted, but he was smart enough to know when the mood was against him. He left the chamber and immediately returned to his office. There he ordered his secretary to dispatch a personal note to Simon Ish Kerioth to make it absolutely clear that he needed to deliver up the necessary evidence before Passover, without fail.

Pressing unusually hard with his ring on the wax seal, his mind was full of anger and intrigue.

'I am holding you personally responsible for making sure this letter finds its way into the hands of Simon Ish Kerioth. Do you understand?' he gave the secretary a steely look, which he knew meant trouble, should anything go wrong.

'Yes, Your Holiness.' The secretary took the sealed scroll and withdrew into the corridor. He decided then and there that he must deliver it personally to Simon, so he quickly made arrangements for a stand in to cover for him while he was away and made preparations to depart to Galilee.

A few days later he arrived with a servant in Capernaum and the two of them made their way to the synagogue to enquire of Simon's whereabouts. The Rabbi was somewhat taken aback by seeing the secretary to the High Priest, and he immediately arranged for his personal servant to wash the Secretary's feet and to make refreshments available.

Seated in his small office, the Rabbi explained that Simon had been staying at the local inn but had not been seen for a few days. 'I gather he was following the man Yeshua from Nazareth. He has caused quite a stir here and great crowds follow him about wherever he goes.

'They say he demonstrates miraculous powers of healing. Some time ago he caused quite a commotion here by apparently casting out an evil spirit right here in our synagogue. Many of our members have gone off after him. It's disturbing, to say the least.'

The Rabbi offered his guest more refreshments, but he declined.

'So where is this Yeshua character at present?' enquired the Secretary.

'I believe he went northwest towards Tyre a few days ago. Whether Simon Ish Kerioth went with him or not, I'm afraid I don't know. You could try the inn. They may have a forwarding address.'

The innkeeper was busy in the small back office behind the reception counter when the secretary entered.

Immediately he got up and came to the counter.

'Can I help you, sir?' he asked.

'I am looking for Simon Ish Kerioth,' replied the secretary.

The innkeeper noticed the secretary's fine garments and realised he was some sort of official from Jerusalem. His accent was a giveaway.

'I believe he may be upstairs in his room. Would you like me to enquire?'

The secretary was pleasantly surprised but tried not to show it.

'Yes please. I will wait here. Oh, and when you've done that, I will need a room for the night and lodgings for the boy. The synagogue will take care of the bill.'

The secretary motioned to his servant to take a seat. The boy took off his back satchel and sat down on a bench by the door.

It was a lovely spring day, and the Secretary looked out of the open door across the sea. Everything seemed very normal and tranquil. No sign of anything unusual. He felt in his pocket for the small scroll he must deliver to Simon.

Just then a door opened, and Simon appeared in the reception area.

'John!' he exclaimed. 'What are you doing here?' He embraced his old friend warmly, much to the discomfort of the secretary, who would have preferred to keep things on a formal footing.

'Is there somewhere private we could talk?' asked the secretary, nervously glancing at the innkeeper.

'I have a room at the back of the inn which is free. You can use that if you like.'

He ushered the pair of them into the back room.

As soon as the door was closed, the secretary explained his business, maintaining a formal atmosphere at all times. He handed Simon the scroll and waited for him to read it.

After opening and reading the scroll, he rolled it back up again and popped it into a pocket in his tunic and sat there, gazing through a slot in the shuttered window.

'Well? What do I report back?'

'Impossible demands!' Simon threw up a hand in the air. 'I can't make him say what he isn't saying, can I?' He paced up and down scratching his neck.

'So why aren't you with him now?' demanded the Secretary.

'I have to write up my notes, otherwise I run out of wax notepads. While I was doing it, he took off up north. As soon as I have finished, I will find him and re-join the group. What more can I do?' Simon asked with a note of despair in his voice.

'You have until Passover to produce the evidence. See to it you don't fail. You know what Caiaphas is like. It's not worth crossing him, as I'm sure you are aware. If you know what's good for you, you'll do it. I don't care what it takes, just do it!'

With that, he turned and left the room without saying goodbye.

Simon stood there thinking. He wondered if the secretary also knew about Judas. Then it suddenly dawned on him that the secretary's father was a distant cousin and close friend of Simon's own father, John. They used to see a lot of each other. Could it be that Simon's father had somehow let the truth about Judas slip out over a little bit too much wine and that Caiaphas had been informed by Simon's own friend, the secretary? It all began to make sense. Simon felt utterly betrayed, but then what did that make him?

He took the scroll out of his pocket and re-read it before rolling it up once more. As he left the little room, he passed a pilot lamp burning in reception. He stopped and touched the scroll against the burning flame, carefully depositing it into the open fireplace and watching the flames until it was all gone. He returned to his room. Tomorrow he would enquire of Yeshua's whereabouts and head north to find him.

Early the following morning Simon stooped to watch through the slats of his bedroom window as the secretary and his servant departed

'So much for friends,' he muttered to himself.

Chapter 11

# THE LIGHT SHINES

The maid was busy dusting the reception area as Simon came down from his room. She stopped, briefly bowing her head and dipping to acknowledge him as he walked through to the small dining room. She put down her duster and followed him. He sat down alone in the room at a small table by the window, the early morning light illuminating the room.

The sun had not quite risen above the mountains beyond the lake of Galilee.

Simon sat looking out of the window across the lake as the maid laid out some fruit and bread before him. Silently she retired.

His mind went over the task in hand. How could he accomplish his purpose? He had felt quite down about it the previous day, but today he felt more positive.

He looked at the food in front of him. The maid had left the room, and he realised that he had not even acknowledged her.

He blessed the food with his customary prayer and in a moment of silence and reflection he recalled Psalm 65, one of his favourites. He remembered singing this particular Psalm as a child at school.

As he uttered the words under his breath, he drew particular comfort from them.

They spoke to him of how the Psalmist had experienced the troubles and the sin of this world and how G_d had forgiven him and blessed him by choosing him to live in his courts and filling him with the good things of his holy Temple. Simon could identify with all of that.

But as he continued, he was struck by a reference to G_d answering us by his awesome and righteous deeds. He particularly noted a reference to his power in stilling the roaring seas, the roaring of the waves; power over nature. Hadn't Yeshua demonstrated such power on the Sea of Galilee? Indeed, he had witnessed deeds of power for himself. The thought made him stop and think.

He returned to the text, but just as he was uttering the words about G_d making the dawn and the sunset shout for joy, something remarkable happened which took him completely by surprise. At the very second that he uttered the words the sun broke over the top of the hills on the far side of the sea and a shaft of intense light pierced the room through the open window. The strength of light grew in a great crescendo of dazzling and almost blinding intensity. It felt as if the whole room was illuminated in every corner.

It was so striking it was almost frightening, but at the same time strangely comforting, and for the first time in all the years of uttering the words of that Psalm he actually felt an overwhelming feeling of joy! It was so intense that he burst out laughing quite involuntarily.

Looking down he could see every detail of the food in front of him, the grain of the wood on the table, the earthenware plate and cup, all in such detail he just sat there in wonder.

As his eyes adjusted to the light it seemed as if for a moment in time all the goodness and abundance of G_d's provision was woven into this spiritual encounter. He could feel the significance of it penetrating his soul, but he couldn't explain it.

Sitting there, drinking in the wonder of that momentary experience, he thought he heard a voice. It wasn't very loud, but it seemed to say, 'I am the light of the world.' 'Was this G_d speaking?' he thought. But the strange thing was, it sounded for all the world like Yeshua's voice.

He did not recall hearing Yeshua say anything like that, and certainly he had not written it down.

Before he could consider the matter further, his thoughts were interrupted by the maid returning with a jug of water. She began to pour some into his cup. As she did so, the sunlight danced invitingly on the flowing water as it trickled into the earthen-ware vessel.

'Thank you,' he said to the maid. She smiled in appreciation and retired. He felt his heart warmly softened with kindness, which he thought was odd, as it was not his usual early morning mood.

# Chapter 12

# MISSION RESUMED

Simon's room in the Inn was a private room; small but functional with a table to write on. There he was able to stretch a scroll out with the two rolled up ends hooked over the front and back of the table top. It wasn't ideal but allowed him to write on what was effectively the outside of the scroll. When rolled up, a blank foot covered the writing and protected it. His friend in the Temple Writing Department had specially developed them for him to use when travelling. His leather carry case contained a number of scrolls inside one another on which he had been recording his evidence. In the bottom of the carry case was a separate compartment for ink and writing equipment. The whole thing was easy to transport and slung neatly over his shoulder with a strap.

Since his expenses were being taken care of through the synagogue, he had been able to enjoy better accommodation than when he travelled on his own account. On those occasions he would use the communal sleeping area, which he shared with all the other travellers. The smell and noise were not to his liking and kept him awake for much of the night, and in some hostels the insect population made sleep nigh impossible.

The inn was largely empty now compared to when Yeshua had been in Capernaum. Then it was completely full, and it was a great relief to Simon that he had been able to spend time at Peter's mother-in-law's. With the help of the many women who followed Yeshua, the food there was excellent, and the conversation was actually with Yeshua rather than just about him.

Simon packed his few possessions into the leather backpack he wore over his shoulders and made ready to depart. He had learned from the innkeeper that Yeshua had recently been seen at Caesarea Philippi, and so he took the road to Bethsaida with a view to finding him to the north.

He felt very much at peace following his experience at dawn and he felt a positive spring in his step. He was looking forward to re-joining the group.

Then it occurred to him that his mission was still unfulfilled and his duty incomplete. With that reality, he felt a strange creeping sadness enveloping him as he walked.

He had only travelled a few miles out of Capernaum when he saw a small cloud of dust rising into the morning air some distance ahead. He didn't want to encounter any trouble, be it with the Roman army or Herod's men, so he left the road and climbed up the bank, taking cover behind some undergrowth where he waited.

As they approached, he could see the familiar outline of the disciples walking along the dusty road with a large group following behind.

At the head of the column was Yeshua, a few strides ahead with a group of disciples keeping the crowd away from him.

Simon returned to the road and waited for the group to approach before joining them as they returned to Capernaum.

At first, he couldn't see Judas, but then he spotted him talking to another man a little way back. He caught up with him and soon learned that they were returning to Capernaum. He asked if they would be staying there a while.

'I've told you before, we never know. We go where Yeshua tells us to, but we don't know what the next move is until he says so.' There was a note of irritation in his voice. Something was not right with Judas.

Simon asked about their time away, but Judas was only able to give him a brief account. He then fell silent as they walked along.

Then Judas turned to Simon.

'He kept going on about how he was going to die. He got very angry with Peter when he tried to tell him that we couldn't let that happen to him. He kept saying things like "The Son of Man is going to be betrayed into the hands of men, and they will kill him and then he will rise from the dead three days later."' He paused. 'What do you think he meant, Uncle Simon?'

Simon thought for a moment, sensing this might be an important opportunity.

'Was he not prophesying?' he enquired.

'Perhaps, but what does it all mean? Here we are returning to Capernaum when we know Herod's men are out to trap him. It's putting everyone in danger. There's still so much for Yeshua to do and it all seems so pointless.'

'Have you not thought that it might be better to work with prophecy than against it? To walk in the path that G_d has set before you, Judas?'

'What? And do the work of the devil? Never! What do you take me for?' Judas was clearly angry with the suggestion.

'But even the devil is subject to the purposes of G_d, is he not?'

Judas looked at Simon. His face was troubled and confused. He said nothing.

Simon went on, 'Haven't you seen how the demons are subject to Yeshua? They have no power to resist him. They must do what they are told, and they know who Yeshua is, don't they?'

Judas just kept walking looking straight ahead without saying a word. They walked on in silence. By now Judas' companion had dropped back and they walked alone. Eventually it was Simon who broke the silence.

'What else has happened?' he asked.

Judas glanced at Simon before answering. 'Privately, we have been discussing who should take over if Yeshua was no longer here. I don't think he knows about it, but we felt it right to be prepared. I think it's between Peter and John, but I'm not sure there's total agreement. Peter's probably the favourite.'

'I see. Well, he's certainly a strong character, I agree. But does that mean that everyone accepts that his prophecy will come true?'

Judas was on guard and said nothing. Shortly afterwards they arrived at Capernaum and were greeted by further crowds lined up along the roadside.

Simon caught Peter's eye and they greeted one another.

'Simon, won't you stay with us tonight? I am sure we can find somewhere for you to bed down in the house.'

'Thank you. It's very kind of you. I would be delighted.'

That evening they ate together and gathered afterwards to listen to Yeshua.

After a short period of silence, when each person was invited to reflect on their time together in Caesarea Philippi, they were ready to hear what Yeshua had to say.

Somewhat to their surprise he put a question to them.

'What were you discussing together while we made our way along the road?'

No one said a word. Their conversation about succession and who should take over seemed badly out of place and they felt embarrassed that such a topic should even have been discussed.

As the silence prevailed, you could have cut the atmosphere with a sword.

Yeshua was unperturbed.

'If you want to be a leader in the Kingdom of G_d, you need to adopt the attitude of a follower, in fact the very least of all the followers; a servant to those you have to lead.'

Sitting behind Peter was his young son Mark, who was peering through a gap in the circle. Yeshua smiled at him and then he invited him to come and sit with him. He drew him onto his lap and enfolded the young boy within his arms.

The boy looked up into the face of Yeshua and they held each other's gaze.

'When you receive one another like this, when you do so in my name, you are receiving me.' He looked up with similar affection at the men and women gathered about him.

Then he looked down at the boy.

'And whoever receives me doesn't just receive me,' he paused, looking up directly at Simon who was listening intently, 'but him who sent me.'

Simon felt distinctly uncomfortable. Not only did he feel the comment was directed at him, but he felt particularly uncomfortable about the way Yeshua was putting himself on a par with G_d Almighty. This did not feel right at all.

Here was Yeshua, not only modelling leadership by suggesting they should behave like servants of the people they were commanding, but that they should treat each other as if they were children! That was clearly not the way that the rest of the world understood leadership, but it was also a thinly veiled criticism of the Jewish hierarchy.

But then to go on and propose that in so doing they were not only receiving him, Yeshua, every time they exercised leadership in this way, but they were actually receiving G_d – this was blatantly blasphemous in its very concept! How dare he?!

Simon was on the verge of taking issue with Yeshua and barely in control, but he knew he needed to keep his head down.

Fortunately, John sensed the developing situation and stepped in by changing the subject. He wanted to know if they had been right to prevent someone who was not a disciple from casting out a demon in Yeshua's name.

Yeshua was emphatic. 'Don't hinder him for there is no one who is going to turn around and speak evil of me after performing a miracle in my name! Put simply, if he's not against us, he's on our side!'

Yeshua looked at his disciples. They were tired. It had been a long day. He looked at Peter's mother-in-law and at Peter's wife, who was standing behind the disciples. They had laid on clean water for their guests to drink when they returned earlier and welcomed them home.

'There is a reward for anyone who so much as gives one of you a cup of water, because you are known as seekers of the Messiah.'

Once again Yeshua turned his attention to Simon Ish Kerioth, who was writing as usual in his wax notebook.

'And whoever causes one of these humble believers to stumble, it would be better if a millstone, so heavy it needs a donkey to turn it, were hung about his neck and he was flung into the sea of Galilee!'

Simon stopped writing and looked up. Did Yeshua know what he was planning to do? Had someone overheard his conversation with Judas? Surely he didn't know – or did he? Who was this man?

By now all eyes were on Simon and he felt very conspicuous. He busily returned to his writing and made as if to write something.

'And if your hand causes you to stumble, cut it off! It's better to be a cripple in the Kingdom of G_d than to go to hell with two good hands!'

Simon took this completely the wrong way. To him it was anathema and against Creator G_d to mutilate your own body. Everyone accepted that a cripple was cursed and had no place in any Kingdom of G_d! It was verging on blasphemy to suggest otherwise. He felt a sense of outrage against what Yeshua was saying. It made him feel determined to bring his mission to a head, partly because he felt afraid that Yeshua somehow was aware of his plan.

But Yeshua was not finished.

He drove home his point, highlighting the same fate for the misuse of one's foot or one's eye in where we walk and what we look at, and finally linking the sinful use of our G_d given assets to a living hell in eternal damnation! He finished by quoting from the last recorded words of Isaiah the prophet, "where their worm does not die and their fire is not quenched!"

There was a stunned silence. Nobody dared to speak.

Yeshua released Peter's son, who returned to his father's side.

The light of the oil lamp next to Yeshua's face bathed him in flickering light, and in the dimness of the gathering gloom he sat there, staring at the ground, as if alone.

He looked up intently at the little flame of the oil lamp.

'You know; everyone will be salted with fire? Salt is good. But if it becomes unsalted, what can you do about it?'

He looked up at his disciples.

'It's important to have salt in yourselves and be at peace with one another.'

With that he blessed them and got up to retire to a place to sleep.

Simon decided not to stay but to take his chances up at the inn by the synagogue. As he walked up the street, he reflected on how the day had begun and what a contrast it had been at its close.

Fortunately, the innkeeper had guessed Simon would be back, and as the synagogue paid him a good rate for the little room, he had taken a chance and reserved it for him, so when Simon entered, he found the innkeeper dozing behind reception; but he was very glad to see him.

Simon lay down in his room and quickly fell into a deep sleep. His dreams were a jumble of events, not making any sense, and early in the morning he awoke with his head in a spin. He lay awake recalling the events of the previous evening. He was sure the teaching of Yeshua was heretical, but how could a heretic do the miracles he did? It was a recurring theme that haunted him. He lay awake for what seemed like an age until finally he fell asleep again.

As a result, he overslept, and the day was well advanced when he arose.

Gathering up his belongings, he hurriedly made his way down to Fisherman's Lane, but the town was eerily empty. When he got there, he discovered from Peter's wife that they had all left very early by boat to cross over to the other side of the sea. Yeshua had decided to go to Batanea, where John the Baptist had been based in his early ministry, an area controlled by the more moderate Phillip, Herod's brother.

Simon hurried down to the port, but all the boats in the entire area were out.

He knew from Judas that the plan was eventually to go up to Jerusalem for Passover, despite the threats. Passover was only a few weeks away. If he took the route around the north of the Sea of Galilee, he would be unlikely to catch up with them in time, and anyway he didn't know how long they planned to spend there or where they planned to visit. He was aware that Yeshua had relatives in the region, but he did not know exactly where they lived.

He had given Judas two sets of wax notepads to use in his absence whenever Yeshua had anything important to say about his Messianic mission or should he perform some important sign.

He made a note of the height of the sun and calculated that there was still time to make it to the first inn on the route back to Jerusalem going south via Samaria, so he set off without further delay.

# PART 2

# EXECUTION

*"Do not go where the path may lead,
go instead where there is no path and leave a trail."*
Ralph Waldo Emerson

# Chapter 13

# BACK TO JERUSALEM

Passing through the familiar Ephraim gate into Jerusalem, with all the sounds and smells that made him feel at home, Simon made his way to his lodgings near the Temple. It was getting late, and he felt tired and hungry.

As he climbed the short flight of steps through the door of his home, he immediately bumped into the maidservant, Anna, who greeted him respectfully. Then, seeing that he had been travelling all day, she offered to prepare him a meal. She had prepared something to eat for one of the other occupants, but he had not returned as expected.

Simon climbed the stone stairway leading to his apartment on the third floor. Opening the door, he entered the darkness, and was greeted by the stale but familiar smell of parchment and ink that he had left behind all those months before. He deposited the scroll case onto the table and his back satchel on the floor and opened the shutters. Fresh air and the evening light refreshed the room.

He slumped down on the chair and removed his sandals. His feet were sore and dirty.

Just then he heard Anna's footsteps in the corridor. She knocked before entering with a bowl, a jug of water and a towel over her arm.

'Thought you might like a bit of a wash after your journey, sir.' She put the bowl down on the floor and knelt down, spreading the towel out on the floor. Having poured some water into the bowl, she began to wash Simon's feet. The cool water was refreshing, and he sat there enjoying the experience.

Anna was in her forties, having been widowed. She had no family, so had taken the position looking after a few senior scribes who lived there. They were often away, so the position was not onerous.

Simon thanked her and asked her if he could have a drink.

She disappeared with the bowl of dirty water, returning shortly with the bowl cleaned, a fresh towel, a small jug of diluted wine and a cup, which she set down on a corner of the table. She poured him a drink, filled the bowl, and withdrew.

Simon blessed the water ceremoniously and removed his tunic before washing his face and hands and splashing water over his upper body and arms. He dried himself and put on a fresh tunic. He sat down feeling very refreshed and combed his hair.

Anna returned. 'Shall I take the bowl?' she asked. 'And would you like me to do some laundry for you, sir?'

'Yes, that would be good. I have a tunic that needs a wash.' He handed her his washing.

Before leaving, she cleared the table to set it out for his meal. As she reached out to pick up the leather scroll case, Simon sprang to his feet.

'I'll take that, if you don't mind,' he said, snatching it away from her.

'I'm so sorry, Sir,' she apologised, 'I didn't mean to offend.'

'That's alright, Anna,' he said, protectively clutching the case to his chest, 'important documents,' he added nonchalantly.

Anna retired, loaded up with his washing and the bowl, before returning later with his meal. Normally Simon would have eaten with the other scribes in the refectory, but as the apartments were largely unoccupied, she served him in his room. In a few days, with Passover approaching, the city would begin filling up and every room would be full.

Many of Simon's friends lived in the Essene quarter of Jerusalem, where women were not permitted to go. They took a dim view of those scribes who lived more centrally and were often attended by female maids. He smiled to himself as he wondered what they would have made of Anna washing his feet – and in his private room!

After eating he retired to his small bedroom and stretched out on his familiar bed. He drew up the blanket over his body and without a further thought fell into a deep and relaxing sleep.

The following morning, he awoke refreshed, albeit a little stiff from his journey.

He locked his door and sat down and took out the scrolls before preparing a report for Caiaphas. He would no doubt have to go and see him because, quite frankly, he had not been able to fulfil his mission.

Reading through the material again, he noted the volume of controversial teaching and remarks. Yeshua often turned Pharisaic teaching on its head. Where the people had been taught for centuries that sickness, disease, and poverty were due to their own sinfulness, he was telling them the opposite. Instead of being the forgotten of G_d, the cursed of this world, he was telling them that in his 'Kingdom of G_d', they were actually in G_d's favour, the blessed, that G_d wanted to touch their lives rather than pass by on the other side of the road. He even quoted the Prophets to back up his argument. Then, just to make matters worse, he would heal them!

Serious though this may be, it was not deserving of the death penalty, which Caiaphas was seeking.

His references to the Prophets implied, quite often, that his mission was the mission of the Messiah. Indeed, it was clear that many of his followers were secretly persuaded that he was the Messiah. What Simon needed was a clear admission or acknowledgement that he was the Messiah, the Son of G_d, and this he did not have, nor did he have it with one other witness to back him up.

Occasionally he had referred to himself as 'The Son of Man', but then so did Ezekiel the Prophet. It was not enough.

In short, he had nothing to give Caiaphas, and that meant trouble.

Passover was a little over two weeks away and Yeshua and his disciples would probably be on their way up to Jerusalem from

Jericho by now. If Judas was able to give him some key evidence, it might help, but would he stand as witness? It was a gamble whether Judas could be persuaded to go ahead with Simon's plan to deliver Yeshua to the authorities.

The scrolls were a key part of the evidence, and Simon knew that while they remained safely in his possession, he had some sort of insurance against Caiaphas taking action against him.

In Simon's bedroom was a secret compartment which he had discovered at the foot of an alcove. He used it to hide money. He bent down and lifted the skirting board, enabling him to remove the short floorboard beneath. There was just enough space for the leather carry case. No one would ever think of looking there.

Instead of writing a report, he decided to try and see Caiaphas that day and explain to him what he was planning to do.

Leaving the scrolls safely hidden away, he left to make an appointment to see Caiaphas.

Sitting in the guard room, waiting for news of an appointment, he was surprised when immediately an orderly came in and ushered him straight up to see the High Priest.

Simon followed the orderly along the covered pathway, nervously rehearsing in his mind what he would say.

Caiaphas was unusually quiet and listened patiently to Simon's plan to persuade Judas to deliver Yeshua up for questioning. It would be up to Caiaphas to extract a confession, and Simon didn't think that would go down well with the High Priest.

Caiaphas rose to his feet and, turning his back on Simon, gazed out of the window towards the Temple with his hands clasped behind his back. It seemed like an age before he spoke.

'It better work,' he said gruffly, turning around to face Simon. 'We are all counting on you for a result, Simon. Failure, you understand, is not an option.'

'Yes, Your Holiness. Believe me, I do understand,' replied Simon nervously.

Simon left with his mind in turmoil. He had been expecting to get a blistering earful from the High Priest. This new mood was disconcerting; even sinister, in fact.

He needed space to think, and he knew only one way of doing that.

He decided to return to the work he had left half finished last year. On the way he realised it was approaching the ninth hour, 3pm, the hour of prayer.

He went up to the Temple and made his way to the area reserved for the scribes and Pharisees. As he knelt, he made confession of his situation to G_d and petitioned for his help. Above all, he wanted to do the right thing.

After prayers he went back to The Old Refectory, to his studio where his work on the scroll of the Psalms lay unfinished. Goodness knows what Rabbi Nathan would be thinking of him, or even if he was still expecting the work he had commissioned. Simon felt a sense of guilt about not letting him know, particularly since it was part paid.

As he entered, the caretaker greeted him like a long-lost friend and handed him a note from Rabbi Nathan. It was asking what had happened to the work. Simon climbed the stairs to his studio and entered. He rolled back the top of his bureau and cleaned out the old ink well before mixing up some fresh ink.

The first thing he did was to write a note to Rabbi Nathan, apologising to him. He left out the fact that he had been staying not far from Nazareth, but tried to explain the delay.

He then retrieved the copy scroll, installing the original above it. Bowing his head, he prepared himself to continue the work by standing respectfully to recite a ritual prayer of purification.

Looking at his work so far, he noted that the last Psalm or Tehillim that he had completed before he departed was Psalm 21. The Psalm proclaims King David's divine deliverance from his enemies. Re-reading it, he feared he might never live to even see the job finished. It was a risk that went with his assignment. But he took comfort from the Psalm.

Carefully annotating the heading for the next Psalm, he spoke the first word out loud before writing it down. The skin was almost invisibly pierced at the start and finish of each line with a small pinprick to guide him accurately across the page.

He had been trained to write with his left hand so that he could move across the paper smoothly without fear of smudging his work. His training had also included means of writing in shorthand so that he could take notes accurately on small fragments of parchment or on wax tablets.

Because each word had to be spoken out loud before writing it down, not only could a scribe maintain a high degree of accuracy, but it also helped to memorise the ancient scriptures. Great care had to be taken, and when it came to writing down the holy name of Jehovah he was required to wash ceremonially before and after committing it to script. It took a while to complete a Psalm, but his practised skill enabled him to finish Psalm 22 by the end of the day.

He had often wondered about this psalm, sitting as it did between a psalm of deliverance and one of triumph. The pain and suffering of King David so graphically depicted seemed incongruous, sandwiched between the two. The King feels abandoned by G_d, taunted, mocked, and tortured. He is almost incredulous at what is happening to him, but he maintains his trust in G_d to save him, redeem him and restore him. His trust is unfailing.

And there it was in verse 28, that the Kingdom is the Lord's and he rules over the nations.

He is vindicated!

When Simon had reached the end, he put down his quill and read through what he had written.

He recalled that Yeshua had talked about suffering death and rising three days later. It had caused so much trouble with the disciples.

He re-read verses 11-18. The pain is particularly graphic, as if the writer is experiencing it, and David is laid in the dust of death. But somehow, he bounces back and there is life...somehow.

His work done for the day, Simon closed up the scrolls, returning them to storage as before.

Tomorrow he would try and get word of Yeshua and Judas.

As he walked home, he noticed how the city was beginning to fill up with people arriving for the Passover festival. Reaching his apartments, even the reception area was full of people. The caretaker was as busy as ever and hardly able to conceal his delight.

'Peace to you, Simon, at this special time of Passover!' he beamed as he greeted him in the hall.

Despite his rather reserved nature, Simon always looked forward to Passover. He found it lifted his spirits, along with everyone else. There was a particularly strong feeling of being one nation despite the Roman occupation.

But as he climbed the stairs, he contemplated the grave issues surrounding his mission, and a sense of disappointment descended on him; this Passover was definitely not going to be a very joyous occasion. He had a lot of work to do.

Chapter 14

# THE PLOT TAKES SHAPE

Later the following day Simon headed east, out of Jerusalem towards the Mount of Olives. He had heard a rumour from the
caretaker that Yeshua and his disciples had returned and had been
seen at a village called Bethany on the outskirts of Jerusalem.
News had spread that they were on their way.

He was just ascending the hill out of the Kidron valley when
he became aware of quite a commotion going on ahead of him
just out of sight.

Hurrying ahead, he was met by a crowd of people coming
towards him. They were cutting branches from either side of the
road and spreading them out along the way. At the head of the
procession was a man riding a donkey. As they got nearer, he
could see that the donkey was a young colt and the person riding it was none other than Yeshua.

It took all of three seconds for his mind to take in what was
unfolding before him in plain sight. Suddenly he realised how
he was going to achieve his objective.

The people around Yeshua were chanting a familiar passage
from Psalm 118. This was a passage and a chant of praise that
ought to be reserved for the Messiah himself!

And there in the middle of it all was Judas, apparently leading the chanting and enthusiastically whipping up the crowd in
praise of the one seated majestically upon the donkey.

It was unthinkable that Judas could have been ignorant of the
significance of what Yeshua was doing.

Yeshua, riding a colt never ridden before, just as would a king
on his own personal transport! Transport on which no one else
was permitted to ride.

Simon could hardly believe his eyes or his good fortune.

The crowd was proclaiming Yeshua as Messiah and Yeshua was doing nothing to stop them.

Simon pushed his way through the crowd and joined Judas. And then, much to the amazement of onlookers, he picked up a branch, waved it triumphantly above his head and joined in the chanting, all the while making sure Judas could see him.

This was risky living, and he knew it.

It was getting late, so having left the colt with its owners and making their way up to the Temple, the crowd began to disperse. Shortly afterwards Yeshua and his disciples left the city, returning to Bethany for the night. Simon joined them on their way back. Judas was ecstatic with excitement.

'Did you see the way everyone was receiving Yeshua, Uncle Simon? They saw him as the one who was going to establish the coming Kingdom! It was fantastic!' he enthused. 'The whole of Jerusalem is behind him! When do you think they will anoint him as King, Uncle Simon?' Simon was concerned about Judas. In his pumped-up state of mind, he might easily cause his carefully hatched plan to implode.

'We will talk about it in the morning, Judas. I will arrange for you to play your part in it all, only be careful not to be heard speaking about it. You can't be too careful. The last thing we want is the Romans getting wind of this, so keep it to yourself, do you understand?' Simon tried to bring Judas back to earth, but he was on such a high that he wasn't sure if he was getting through. 'I will meet you in the Temple tomorrow. I have to meet Caiaphas early in the morning, but I will come to the Temple mid-day and meet you there. We can find a quiet place to talk over the plan.' They parted company and Simon returned to his apartment.

The following day Simon made his way to Caiaphas' house early. He was now confident he could rescue his reputation.

Caiaphas was seated behind his desk as usual, surrounded with the affairs of his position.

'Take a seat, Simon.' He motioned towards the pile of cushions on the floor without raising his head. Simon sat uncomfortably on the edge of the pile.

'Thank you for seeing me at such short notice, Your Holiness,' he began, but Caiaphas raised his hand without looking up and Simon's voice tailed off.

Moments later the High Priest set down his quill and rolled up the small scroll he was writing in, sealing it with wax and imprinting it with his official seal. He rang the small bell on his desk and the secretary appeared. He glanced at Simon but said nothing.

He was about to instruct him to take the scroll to the intended recipient but stopped short, looking at Simon, before taking up his quill and writing the name of the recipient on the outside.

'Take this to the addressee,' he said, handing the scroll to the secretary. 'Make sure you don't discuss this with anyone. That's an order.'

The secretary backed out, clutching the scroll, without even acknowledging Simon.

Simon was wondering who the recipient might be but Caiaphas, noticing his interest, put him at ease.

'Nothing to do with you, Simon,' he said, 'but come, tell me why you are here. Do you bring me some good news?' He sat down on the cushions and seemed to be unusually friendly. His mood swings always made Simon feel nervous.

'Well actually I do, Your Holiness. I think everything is now in place.'

'After yesterday's performance, I most certainly hope so,' he changed his mood again. 'So, what's your plan exactly?' he added with an obviously fake smile.

'I have persuaded my neph...' he quickly corrected himself, denying Caiaphas the chance to deride him, 'I have persuaded Judas to accept that he will play a part in the destiny of our nation by delivering up Yeshua to you, Your Holiness, so that you can anoint him King over Israel.' Caiaphas raised an eyebrow as if he was not supposed to take it seriously. 'Of course, not that you will *actually* do it, Your Holiness, but he *believes* you will.' he corrected himself. 'His understanding is that once you have anointed Yeshua, he will be enabled to use his great power to lead the nation to victory over the Romans.' Simon waited for the response.

'Hmm. But according to you he preaches nonviolence – "love your enemies" I think you mentioned in your report.'

Simon thought for a moment. He wasn't expecting that response.

'Maybe instead he could bring about a peaceful agreement where the Romans withdrew of their own volition.' Caiaphas didn't look convinced. 'Or perhaps he could bring about some sort of natural disaster from G_d to cause them to withdraw.' Was he clutching at straws?

'And why,' asked Caiaphas, testing the plan, 'if that's what this plan is supposed to deliver, and with you and Judas acting as intermediaries, does he not just walk in here and give himself up? It could easily be arranged, don't you agree?' But then, realising his error, he corrected himself. 'But I rather think he's not going to do that, is he?'

Caiaphas scratched his beard, continuing, 'But the thought of arresting him in a public place would be a disaster, judging by what happened yesterday. His public support is growing daily, and with so many of his supporters flooding into Jerusalem for Passover, there would be a riot. It's out of the question.'

'No, we are going to have to arrest him away from the public gaze, like after dark, but we need to know where he is going to be, and we need to be able to clearly identify him.'

The two men thought for a moment.

'May I suggest, Your Holiness, that Judas, being one of his close disciples, will know where they go each night?' Simon was always quick to vary a plan.

Caiaphas still had some doubts. 'But we want to make sure we arrest the right man in the dark. It's unlikely that any of my men will know what he looks like in the dark. We're only going to get one strike at this.'

'Yes, I see Your Holiness, but Judas knows him well enough to identify him in the dark.'

'But how will he communicate that to my men without raising suspicion?' thought Caiaphas. 'Perhaps Judas could go up to him and greet him personally,' he suggested.

Simon agreed.

'May I suggest, Your Holiness, that we arrange a meeting to-night after dark with Judas to persuade him of our plan? I think he would need the reassurance that you are going to anoint Yeshua king over Israel in the Temple. I can bring him here myself. I have arranged to meet him later today.' Caiaphas looked at him apprehensively.

'So, you want me to see Judas and tell him I'm going to anoint Yeshua king over Israel, and then Judas will lead us to Yeshua in the middle of the night accompanied by an armed guard? Is that what you are suggesting? Isn't he going to be a bit suspicious of the armed guard?'

'Not at all, Your Holiness. The guard could be for Yeshua's protection. They could be seen to be the foundation of his new army.'

'So how many men do we take? About 50, do you think?'

'I think it would need to be as big as you could make it, Your Holiness. Do you have enough to make up a cohort of 600 men?' asked Simon tentatively.

'600 men! Are you completely out of your mind? That's the entire Temple Guard! And what? To arrest one man?'

'It does need to look authentic, Your Holiness.'

Simon waited while Caiaphas thought it through. Caiaphas found Simon's plans unnerving, as they twisted and turned with every suggestion. But he could see how it might work. He thought about timing and the Passover. He could get the Sanhedrin to-gether, but then Yeshua would need to go before the Roman Governor Pontius Pilate as well as Herod. There was a lot to or-ganise and not much time to do it in. It all hinged on Judas be-ing convinced. He could see that.

While he was thinking, Simon was also having a thought. As usual, he was worried that the whole operation might end up as his idea and therefore his fault. And if Caiaphas was seen to be behind it, it would undoubtedly be he, Simon, who would end up taking the blame. What he needed was convincing evi-dence that would lead people to believe that Judas was acting of his own volition and was the sole betrayer; something that would seriously implicate him.

As he thought, it occurred to him that if there was a monetary consideration for handing Yeshua over it would look like a straightforward business transaction between Caiaphas and Judas, rather than an evil deception by Simon. The problem was that it would be difficult to persuade Judas to ask for money or even accept it. He would need to be persuaded that there was another important reason to ask for money.

Again, his scheming mind went to work.

Perhaps Judas could be persuaded that he needed to test the genuine motives of Caiaphas to see if this was a deception or not. If Caiaphas was really with this plan to anoint Yeshua as King, Judas could test it by asking how much he valued the work.

He explained all of this to Caiaphas, who accepted the plan. As far as he was concerned, all that mattered was that he got the chance to arrest Yeshua and away from the public gaze, and any plan that produced that result was good enough for him. He wasn't really interested in how it would work.

Simon left to meet Judas in the Temple as planned.

As he approached the Outer Court of the Temple, he became aware of a commotion coming from the inside. What he saw caught him quite by surprise.

As usual, at the entrance to the Outer Court there were tradesmen selling various live sacrificial offerings, with money changers exchanging common currency for Temple currency and many other traders selling their wares to the many visitors entering the Temple. The place was packed with people.

Suddenly he could see Yeshua shouting at them and physically turning over their tables and furniture, scattering money, caged birds, and other wares all over the floor. It was chaos. Dust, feathers, and coins went flying in every direction. Stallholders were shouting in protest and trying to rescue their property and possessions. Doves and other small birds were taking advantage of their unexpected freedom while the people were egging Yeshua on with loud supportive cheers of encouragement. They were loving it.

For as long as anyone could remember, these traders had been providing a so called 'service' to the people and paying a percentage to the Temple, and in so doing ripping off the public, who were paying for it all from their hard-earned savings.

As Simon approached, it looked as if a very ugly situation was unfolding, with the Temple Guard stepping forward, awaiting orders to intervene. But with so much popular support, the authorities were reluctant to use force, for fear of triggering a riot.

'Go on Yeshua!' cried one man. 'Give them what they deserve!' The crowd went wild cheering him on.

When Yeshua had made his point, he called for calm and began to speak to the people about the sanctity of the Temple as a place of prayer. He used quotes from Isaiah and Jeremiah to support his case against making it a den of thieves.

Simon watched with interest. This was not the Yeshua he had come to know in Galilee. This looked increasingly like the sort of Messiah figure that would fit his plan perfectly. He watched Judas, who was standing very close to Yeshua and taking in every word.

Just then, he caught Judas' eye. Judas worked his way through the crowd.

'Did you see what Yeshua did, Uncle Simon?' he asked excitedly. 'I'm beginning to see where his works are leading him!' He beamed from ear to ear. Simon said nothing but smiled back, nodding in agreement. He took Judas by the elbow, guiding him away from the crowd.

'Come. I will introduce you to someone who will enable you to fulfil your plans.'

Together they made their way out and down towards Caiaphas' house.

Judas was brimming with all the events surrounding their return to Jerusalem and didn't seem that bothered about where he was going.

Suddenly Simon stopped and pulled him to one side. He thought he better warn him where they were going.

'We're going to see Caiaphas,' he said. Judas looked appalled.

'Caiaphas? Why are we going to see Caiaphas, Uncle Simon?' There was more than a note of apprehension in his voice.

Simon led Judas off the main street, down a narrow alley way that opened out into a small square. The two men sat down on a low wall in the centre.

'You remember what I told you about anointing Yeshua as King?' He had dropped his voice so as not to be overheard. He looked around anxiously. 'Well, without going into too much detail here and now, I can tell you that I have cleared the plan at the very highest level and everything is set to go.' Simon looked at Judas intently, taking hold of both arms.

'Judas, you have been chosen to fulfil your destiny. Your name will go down in history as the man who enabled our nation, and indeed the world, to be saved.'

'But why me?' asked Judas, 'Why not Peter or John? They are surely the more senior disciples, are they not?'

'I don't know the mind of G_d,' said Simon, 'who can tell why the last should be first?' This rang a bell with Judas, who recalled Yeshua using the same phrase.

'You need to recognise your destiny, Judas. Each of us has a calling from G_d. We need to act when the time comes. And you have been called for such a time as this.'

Judas just sat there looking at Simon.

He felt a whole range of emotions. He felt flattered, he felt honoured, he felt anxious and apprehensive, and he felt afraid. Back in Galilee it had all seemed so remote, but here in Jerusalem it felt very different, imminent, real, and dangerous.

Simon could instinctively see what was going on in Judas' head. He could see there was a battle going on for his very soul. He could not afford to let him back-off at this stage.

'Yeshua needs you to do this for him.' He urged Judas on. 'Why do you think he chose you as his disciple? Was it just to use you to keep the purse? Are you not a part of his great plan to usher in the Kingdom of G_d?'

Judas felt confused. He wanted to do what was right, but this was too big for him. He lacked confidence. There were times when he just wished it would all go away.

Simon felt the time had come for a change of tactics. He needed to present the plan as a fait accompli.

'What's going to happen is this...' he paused to make sure Judas was taking this in. 'The High Priest is going to make available a large body of Temple Guards who will ensure nothing happens to Yeshua until he is safely brought back to him. They will enable the High Priest to carry out his great plan. Then, just as our forefathers were miraculously delivered from the tyranny of the Egyptians at the time of the very first Passover, so Yeshua will be released to deliver Israel from the tyranny of the Roman Empire.'

'So, what do you need me for?' interrupted Judas. 'Why doesn't Yeshua just go along with the plan?' Simon could see where this was going, but ignored it.

'Your task is simply to identify Yeshua as your Master to the Captain of the Guard. The whole operation will take place under cover of darkness so as not to raise any suspicions and also to return Yeshua unhindered to the High Priest. You are needed to assist the Captain by identifying Yeshua to him. How else will he know who he is?'

Judas nodded. It did make sense and seemed fairly straight forward.

'Now,' Simon continued, 'there is a small matter that remains. Nothing to worry about, but the High Priest will need to know that you will not let him down. He needs some assurance from you.'

'How do I do that?' asked Judas.

'What I suggest is that you must ask him how much he'll pay you to carry out this work for him. It's just a formality, you understand, but he will expect you to seek a reward for your services. It's the way things are done in these circles.'

Judas did not like the sound of that. 'You mean I need to sell Yeshua to them? That's what you mean, isn't it?' Judas' reaction was understandable, but it caught Simon by surprise. For one horrible moment, he could see the whole plan unravelling and coming to nothing. He tried to remain calm and reassure Judas. He felt so close, he must use all his devious ingenuity to carry this one off. He took a deep breath.

'Judas,' he said slowly pretending to be irritated, 'it's just a formality. They probably won't even offer you anything, but at least you'll have done the right thing by asking and they'll feel reassured that you're going to do this for real, that you're committed not to let them down. It demonstrates your credibility, Judas, and sets all the arrangements on a sound footing.'

Judas felt comforted, although still a bit ill at ease, but he trusted his uncle and was prepared to go along with the suggestion.

Simon breathed deeply. 'Come on, we need to go.'

He took him by the arm and the two men left for their rendezvous.

Chapter 15

# IN THE TEMPLE

Caiaphas was standing in the middle of his office as Simon and Judas entered. With his back to the window, he was in silhouette against the light, so Judas could not see his face properly. It made him feel even more nervous than he felt before he came in. But Caiaphas turned on his charm, greeting the two men warmly and offering them some refreshments. He motioned for them to sit down and invited them to make themselves comfortable. Simon led the way and Judas followed.

They were not alone, being in the company of two other official looking men who also greeted them warmly but said nothing more.

'Simon has told me all about you Judas. You are a credit to your family and the whole nation.' Caiaphas tried to make Judas feel more at home, although he had a long way to go.

'Thank you, Your Holiness,' replied Judas politely.

'Now, this is a busy time for all of us with Passover coming up, so let's get down to the business in hand, shall we?' Caiaphas skipped the formalities and got straight to the point.

'I gather, Judas, that you are in on the plan for Yeshua and that you are agreeable to helping us establish that plan?'

'Yes, Your Holiness.' There was a pause.

'Good,' replied Caiaphas slowly, and there was an awkward silence while Caiaphas looked at Simon and Simon looked at Judas, raising his eyebrows and nodding encouragingly as if to urge Judas on.

Judas stumbled over his words, 'What are you willing to give me to deliver Yeshua to you?' he asked falteringly. His heart was beating so hard it was distracting him.

Judas glanced at Simon, who smiled approvingly.

'Of course!' responded Caiaphas and gestured to the two officials who were watching in bemusement but seemed to be prepared for the question. One of them produced a small bag while the other reached up and took down a set of scales from a table next to him. After testing the scales empty for accuracy, they proceeded to empty the contents of the bag carefully onto one of the trays while selecting the relevant weight to put on the other. The scales seesawed back and forth satisfactorily.

'Thirty shekels of silver,' the official announced, before lifting the dish of silver and emptying it back into the bag. He pulled the cord tight, securing it with a knot before handing it to Judas.

No one said a word until Caiaphas broke the silence.

'You will come to us before the Passover when you are able to identify where Yeshua will be and will accompany us there, where you will identify him to the Captain of the Guard, and he will accompany him safely back here to me.' Caiaphas gave him a reassuring smile and the officials nodded in agreement.

'Are there any questions?'

'How will I identify him to the Captain?' asked Judas.

'I suggest you just greet him as you normally do.' Caiaphas looked around the assembled gathering.

'It's been a pleasure meeting you, Judas,' concluded Caiaphas, rising to his feet. Simon guided Judas out. As he left, Judas glanced at the small table with some wine and silver cups untouched. It had all happened so fast they had not even had time to drink it.

Once out in the street they made their way back to the Temple via Simon's apartment.

Judas could feel the weight of the silver in his inner pocket. Even though it was less than a pound in weight, it seemed to weigh heavily as he walked.

Normally, such a large sum of money in his pocket would have made him feel good. Just the weight of it, dragging his tunic down, would have given him a good feeling, but it felt very different on this occasion. It was like a sort of dead weight. He felt confused.

'When the time is right you know where to find me.' Simon gestured to his lodgings as they passed by on their way up to the

Temple. 'In the meantime, do not discuss this with anyone. Do you understand, Judas? Not with your fellow disciples or even with Yeshua. It is vital that nobody interferes with the plan and tries to change the course of history or undo your destiny.'

Judas gave Simon a long hard look. He had a strange feeling that events were running away with him. He didn't quite know how to deal with the confusing thoughts that seemed to be engulfing him.

Jerusalem was bustling with people from far and wide. The noise and smell were most disagreeable. They both disliked crowds, but the closer they got to the Temple the worse it became.

By the time they arrived the authorities had mustered a sizeable number of learned Pharisees and others who would be able to confront Yeshua and his popular teaching. Having formed a plan together, they made their move.

They had managed to secure the services of Elazar, one of the former High Priests. Although getting on in years, his mind was still as sharp as a dagger. The group approached Yeshua, pushing their way through the crowd, who obediently stepped aside to let them through.

Elazar cleared his throat loudly. People looked around.

'Some of your deeds are remarkable,' he began, 'but tell us, who *authorises* you to do these things?' He strung out the word 'authorises' to make it absolutely clear that he, Elazar, and the other High Priests had nothing to do with authorising Yeshua. So, by what authority *was* he acting?

Yeshua saw straight through the question. He paused and then took a few steps forward towards Elazar who, aware of Yeshua's confrontation with the traders, began to look a little uncomfortable. What was he going to do?

'I'll tell you what,' said Yeshua, turning around to face the crowd as if in a courtroom, 'why don't I ask you a question and then if you can answer me, I will tell you by what authority I do "these things," as you put it?'

No one spoke. Yeshua was visibly in charge.

Elazar had no idea what was coming next. He was no fool and it began to dawn on him that he was about to be caught in his own trap.

Turning to face Elazar, Yeshua spoke.

'Let's talk about authority, shall we? Was the baptism of John the Baptist from heaven or...' he paused, '... or from men? Answer me that?' he declared with a broad smile.

Ouch! Elazar turned to his companions with a begging look. Simon was standing not far away and heard the exchange.

'If we say from heaven then he will say "Why didn't you believe him?" and we can't say "From men,"' the tall Pharisee looked around at the waiting crowd, 'if we do that, what will the people say? There are too many of his followers here. They'll not take kindly to such an answer.'

The exchange went on in a low whisper. Finally, they realised they had no alternative. Elazar turned back to Yeshua, who was patiently awaiting his response.

'We don't know.' he said feebly.

Yeshua turned to the crowd, exposing their 'don't know' as a 'won't say' and calmly telling the crowd, 'Then neither will I tell you by what authority I do "these things."' The crowd loved it, cheering wildly.

Elazar awkwardly re-joined his companions.

Judas gave Simon's sleeve an excited tug. 'Did you see that! Surely the time is nearly ready? Shall we do it now, Uncle Simon?'

'I don't think this is the appropriate moment Judas, there are too many people about.' He took Judas by the arm and led him forward. 'Let's listen to what Yeshua is teaching, shall we?'

Yeshua had begun to tell a story about a vineyard owner. Simon recognised that the parable was based on a passage from the fifth chapter of Isaiah. It was a story intended to embarrass the authorities and portrayed the villain as the caretakers of the vineyard, clearly pointing the finger at Israel.

Elazar and the other Pharisees slipped away, but not for long.

About twenty minutes later another group of Pharisees appeared, accompanied by some scribes known to be loyal to Herod, and made their way forward.

One of the Herodian's, an Essene in his long white robe addressed Yeshua. 'Teacher,' he respectfully began, catching Yeshua's attention, 'Teacher, we know you are truthful, deferring to no man, not partial to anyone because we have heard you teaching the way of G_d in truth.' He made sure the crowd were listening before continuing. 'Is it lawful to pay the Poll tax to Caesar or not?'

This was a devilishly cunning question.

Yeshua made no reply. A swallow swooped low over the heads of the crowd. You could hear the air flowing over her wings above the hush that had descended upon the crowd.

Yeshua lifted his head to watch it pass. You could see a slight movement in his lips, and he closed his eyes momentarily.

He turned to the questioner, who was looking decidedly pleased with himself.

This was a truly cunning trap. The look on his face betrayed the pride he felt that it was he who had thought of it. He went on. 'Shall we pay, or shall we *not pay*?' He drew out the last words with undisguised pleasure.

Yeshua looked long and hard at him. The Essenes had been his friends, so why this hostility?

'Why are you testing me?' he asked in a warm and submissive tone. He turned to the crowd. 'Does anyone have a denarius?' he asked. 'I just want to look at it.' This was the coin required to be paid as the poll tax and amounted to a day's pay for a soldier.

Someone nearby handed him the coin and he studied it closely, turning it over in his hand. It was only a small coin, but it had the image of Tiberius clearly imprinted on one side with a shorthand inscription which read, 'Ti Caesar Divi Avg F Avgvstvs' (Caesar Augustus Tiberius, son of the Divine Augustus).

He moved closer to his questioner who by now was looking somewhat less confident.

Yeshua held it up in such a way that his questioner could see the small image of the Emperor on the coin. 'Whose image is this?' he asked, 'And the inscription?'

The Essene looked at the coin carefully. 'Caesar,' he replied.

Yeshua continued to hold up the small coin. His hand still obscured his face from view. 'So, give to Caesar what belongs to him.'

Then he slowly lowered the coin and, as he did so, the Essene was left looking full into the face of Yeshua. The original question rang in his ears: '*Whose image is this and the inscription?*'

Yeshua continued. 'And give to G_d the things that belong to G_d.' He handed the coin back to its owner. Meanwhile the full implication of what he had just said began to sink in.

The crowd erupted!

The Essene just stood there, transfixed, trying to take in what he had just seen and heard. He didn't really hear the crowd; all he was aware of was the image before him. There was no malice in those eyes. But just whose image was he really looking at? His friends took him by the arm and drew him gently away.

Simon was also transfixed, his stylus in one hand and wax pad in the other. He gradually came to and busily wrote down what he had just heard, but nothing could describe what he had just seen. Once again, he had given a living testimony as to who he was without actually saying so.

All afternoon Yeshua taught the crowd and took questions with great wisdom and authority.

Simon had been listening and hastily noting down every word, but nothing Yeshua had said had been evidence of any value. But he began to realise that he was quite enjoying his teaching. It was refreshingly different to anything he had heard before.

Then there was a brief lull in the questions. Simon had been sitting on a stone bench that ran around the outside of the Inner Court. He closed his wax notebook and put away his stylus before standing up and approaching Yeshua.

'May I ask a question?' he ventured. Yeshua turned to listen.

'What would you say is the number one commandment, Rabbi?' he asked respectfully.

Yeshua smiled. 'The first commandment is addressed to Israel. The Lord our G_d is one Lord,' he replied looking him up and down. Simon's facial features, his long white robes, his greying beard tumbling down over his breast and his hair tied back in a white headscarf were quintessentially Jewish.

Yeshua continued, 'And love the Lord your G_d with everything you are; your heart, soul, mind and strength. And there is one more Simon. You must love your neighbour as if you were loving yourself. I guess there really isn't anything to top these two great commandments.'

Simon immediately recognised the two commandments straight out of the Torah in Deuteronomy and Leviticus.

Simon smiled back at him.

'Spot on, Teacher!' he replied, and then, not to be outdone, he added, 'That's right, because by saying he is one, that means there really isn't anyone other than him. So loving him with all one's heart, intellect and strength takes you beyond all the burnt offerings ever made.'

Simon's knowledge of the scriptures impressed Yeshua, and in particular his application of the truth. But Yeshua stopped smiling. His face became quite stern and earnest. He took a step closer to Simon and gave him one of those heart-searching looks. And then he said to him in a soft voice that only Simon could hear, 'I do believe there's only one more step to take and you too will find yourself in the Kingdom!' Yeshua turned on his heel and, addressing the crowd, he lifted his voice again.

'You know; I have a question about the Messiah.' The crowd fell particularly silent. The Messiah was definitely a taboo subject in public.

'The Scribes say that the Messiah is the Son of David. But David himself said, whilst under the power of the Holy Spirit, "The Lord said to my Lord, sit at my right hand until I turn all your enemies into a footstool!" Do you remember?

'So, if David himself calls the Messiah "Lord", how come he is his son?' Yeshua held out his hands and shrugged his shoulders, puckering his lower lip as if to say, 'He can't be, can he?'

Although the crowd loved it when Yeshua made fools of the authorities, he warned them not to be fooled or to try and imitate them.

The day was drawing to a close and the crowds were drifting away. Yeshua joined Simon on the stone bench opposite the Treasury. Considering what he had been planning for Judas to do, Simon thought he might ask him about his reference to 'one more step,' but then he thought better of it. Yeshua was so relaxed that Simon wondered if he had any idea what he had been plotting with Caiaphas.

People were filing past, putting their offerings in the collection box on their way out.

Then a widow caught Yeshua's attention. Dressed all in black, she was among the last to leave.

'Did you see that?' he exclaimed. His disciples were beginning to get a bit jumpy. They didn't want to be left on their own in the Temple area without the comfort of the crowd. The widow had just put a couple of coppers into the box, and together they amounted to nothing. What was so significant about that? they thought.

'I'll tell you what,' he said, 'that woman has just donated more money than all the rest of these people put together. You see, these people have simply put in some of their surplus income, but she is remarkable. She has no one to look after her and she just put in everything she has! Now she has nothing left to live on; nothing!' Simon felt a bit uncomfortable, as he had not put anything in at all.

The disciples watched the woman depart, wondering how much longer they need delay their departure.

Yeshua stood up, with no sense of urgency. He turned to Peter. 'Now that's what I call true giving! Shall we go then?'

Everyone looked greatly relieved and hurriedly joined those leaving the Temple. No one said a word. As they were leaving, Peter looked up nervously at the impressive architecture and remarked at the size of some of the blocks of stone.

'Have you ever seen such a huge building, Teacher?'

Yeshua stopped and surveyed the sight of Herod's spectacular building work. The party looked around nervously, wishing Peter would keep his thoughts to himself.

'Do you see these impressive buildings, Peter? Well, it may interest you to know that not one stone will be left standing on another. The whole lot is going to be torn down.' He spoke quite nonchalantly, looking at Peter.

Those around including the disciples gasped. Simon also heard it and quickly made a note in his wax notepad, writing down the comment.

By now the disciples were feeling really nervous. Everyone who overheard his comment were mumbling to themselves disapprovingly, including one or two officials who were overseeing the departure of the public.

Peter cleared his throat. "Teacher, I think we ought to get going, it's getting late.'

They were staying at Bethany, just outside Jerusalem, to the east, so they headed home. On the way there, Yeshua stopped on the Mount of Olives to watch the sun setting over the Temple. He began to explain in more detail some things concerning the 'End Times' as he saw it. Simon went with them, but as the sun went down, he returned to his lodgings in Jerusalem. As he made his way home, he reflected on the day. Would this be the last time he would hear Yeshua's teaching? He didn't know, but he had a feeling in the pit of his stomach that it might well be the last.

Lying back on his bed that night he recalled what Yeshua had said to him about taking 'one more step' and he would be in the Kingdom. Was he referring to the next step to hand him over to the authorities, that he would actually do something of a political nature, or did he have something else in mind? You could never tell with this man! There was no doubt that the next few days would reveal the truth, he thought.

A moment later he was asleep, but his sleep would not be satisfying that night. He was aware of a recurring dream which he had been having lately, but once awake he was unable to recall it.

# Chapter 16

# THE DEED IS DONE

Caiaphas was getting impatient. He had received no word from Simon as to where and when he would be able to arrest Yeshua. It was now Monday and there were only a few days to go before the Passover. It was getting close.

What was going wrong? Why was he being kept in the dark? It would soon be too late. He had to do something.

It was already late afternoon when he decided to convene a meeting of the Lesser Sanhedrin at his Palace. Couriers were dispatched with an urgent summons to an emergency meeting. Many members had already started preparations for their evening meal when they received their summons.

As members filed into the chamber there was a lot of grumbling. People were asking what all the urgency was about.

Caiaphas addressed the meeting.

'I've called this meeting because time is running out on us to arrest this Galilean troublemaker, Yeshua of Nazareth, and to nip his rebellious plot to overthrow our administration in the bud. We need to act now. We can't wait any longer. Our intelligence is that he is planning to make his move very shortly and I intend to act ahead of any move.'

There were mumbles of approval from many and several spoke up for immediate action.

Joseph of Arimathea interrupted, calling for calm. In his opinion there was little evidence that this Yeshua was planning a political coup, but others cited his staged entry into Jerusalem blatantly demonstrating his intent to associate himself with the Messiah. He had shown no restraint on his disciples and made no attempt to correct the crowd who were proclaiming him King.

But there was little support for direct action at Passover, with the city bursting at the seams with travellers from all over the known world. They noted the public support associated with this man and warned against doing anything that would trigger a public riot. They felt it would play directly into Pontius Pilate's hands to initiate a backlash of indiscriminate violence on the people. Some of these members had been present in the Temple and had witnessed how easily he was able to whip up public support against the authorities to further his popularity.

The debate raged until, almost unnoticed, a guard appeared at the door of the chamber and signalled to Caiaphas. Caiaphas left his seat and went to the door to speak with the guard. After a few words he returned to his seat standing up and raising his hand for quiet.

'I think we have a solution at last,' he announced, 'but I want you to be on standby in the next day or so to reconvene a full meeting of the Council. The meeting is now closed, and you are dismissed.'

And with that he departed into a side room where Simon and Judas were waiting. The two men followed Caiaphas to his office.

Judas had just left a meal in Bethany with Yeshua and the rest of the Disciples. Part of what had taken place at the meal had spurred him on to take action now.

He had found himself in turmoil in recent days, unable to finalise in his mind what sort of Messiah Yeshua really was. One minute he was riding into Jerusalem like a King in waiting and the next he was teaching the crowds in the Temple in his old familiar style, albeit with more direct authority. The next minute he was talking about coming in great power and glory at some stage in the future with all the angels of heaven in order to gather the elect from all over the world and to establish his rule and authority. It was very confusing for him. He had thought to discuss it directly with Yeshua, but there was no opportunity to speak to him alone. Everything was moving so quickly.

But then during the meal, there was a woman who entered with a very expensive jar of pure Nard ointment. She was well known to everyone, but no one said a word. Then she poured the whole contents all over Yeshua, starting with his head down to his feet; the aroma was so overpowering it filled the entire house.

At first Judas had been somewhat taken by surprise and felt indignant that such a valuable quantity of perfume should have been so extravagantly wasted, when it could have been sold and the money used to alleviate poverty.

But then Yeshua had made it very clear that what she had done was to him a very beautiful deed; anointing his body for burial.

Yeshua had been talking for some time about his suffering and death. How he would be delivered into the hands of men who would kill him, but that three days later he would come back from the dead.

Suddenly Judas could see it all. He could make sense of it *powerful mindset* in his own mind. He could see how Yeshua would be anointed King by the High Priest and that there would be a huge uprising against the Romans. Yeshua would be seized and killed but he would come back to life in the biggest miracle of all time. That he would utterly bewilder the enemy with this astonishing feat of power going on to overthrow their rule and driving them out of the region altogether. He had made up his mind to play his part in this great and divine plan.

In Caiaphas' office the discussion centred around the plan to detain Yeshua. Simon did the talking to make sure that Judas was not alerted to the true nature of the detention.

Two days later, Yeshua sent his disciples out to make ready a venue for them to celebrate the Passover meal together. Yeshua, in typical fashion, briefed the advance party as to precisely what they would encounter, and true to form they saw a man carrying a pot of water on his head which he had just collected from the Gihon spring. Clearly this was normally women's work, so he was not hard to spot. In fact, he was making his way back to the male only Essene quarter where women were not allowed.

They were to follow him back to where he was staying and to tell the owner of the house that 'the Teacher wants to know where the guest room is so that his disciples can use it to prepare a Passover meal for them to eat together.'

Once again, they found everything exactly as described on the top floor, all ready and waiting for them to use. Just like the colt tied up, these devout people didn't just believe the Teacher would come, they had actually made preparations for him. So it was the most natural thing in the world for them to make available the things they had prepared.

That day lambs were being slaughtered for the Passover. Most of them had been born on the hillsides of Bethlehem where Yeshua had also been born. They too had been brought to Jerusalem to be sacrificed. Passover was a time to remember when the blood of firstborn lambs was daubed on the doorposts of the enslaved Israelite homes in Egypt to alert the Angel of Death to pass over that house and thus save their firstborn sons from death. Thus, they escaped into the promised land through the Red Sea, the desert wilderness and then over the waters of the Jordan.

Would history be about to repeat itself on a universal scale in a divine twist?

The thought never occurred to the two disciples who followed the man with the pitcher of water that day, one of whom carried the purse to buy the things they needed that evening.

It was during that fateful meal that Yeshua made it known to those who were listening that one of them would betray him. It was done quite openly, and he even went as far as to tell them who it was by turning to his left and sharing part of the meal with Judas, who was occupying the traditional position of guest of honour on the left of the host. Judas felt affirmed in his master's choice, he felt a power come over him. Was it the power of destiny?

When Yeshua invited Judas to sit in the place of honour, on his left, it did not go unnoticed by Peter. He could hardly believe his eyes. He said nothing, but instead deliberately went and reclined in the place normally reserved for the servant, at the bottom of the table. He would wait and see if Yeshua would move him up to the place of honour, an act of humility which he had once taught his disciples to observe. Later, Yeshua would teach Peter what being a servant really meant, but for the moment he had other things on his mind.

So, during the course of the meal, it came as no surprise that Yeshua, aware of what was happening to Judas, turned and said to him, 'What you are about to do, do it quickly.' For Judas this remark was like a green light for him to go and fulfil his destiny.

As Judas rose to his feet the others assumed he was being sent out on a buying errand.

With those words echoing in his head, Judas made his way to Caiaphas' house as planned, where he met up with Simon, who was waiting for him in the guard room.

Together they talked as they made their way to Caiaphas' office.

The door was opened by a young servant, and they were ushered in. There was one other person present with Caiaphas that evening. It was the Captain of the Temple Guard.

Pleasantries and introductions were exchanged but nothing much was said as Judas was escorted out with the captain to a rear entrance, where they met up in the street with the rest of the Temple Guard and others. Simon went with them.

Judas had to pass beside these soldiers, many of whom carried burning torches. Their rugged faces were illuminated as he squeezed by but showed no emotion as they peered at him from under their helmets.

Judas knew where Yeshua and the disciples would be. They had been using an old olive grove called Gethsemane to meet after dark, where they would remain until they felt it safe to return to their accommodation. Yeshua would pray while the others would keep watch and pray. Located just beyond the Kidron valley at the base of the Mount of Olives, it was partway between where they were staying and Jerusalem. It was a perfect location to look up towards the Old City and the Temple and to be safe alone without distraction.

Judas took up his position at the front of the column alongside the captain, who immediately gave the order to advance. Not a word was said as they descended down into the Kidron Valley and up towards the garden.

Yeshua was preparing himself for the start of his ordeal, but the eleven disciples were unaware of what was about to happen.

As they approached the entrance everyone was especially quiet. They all had their orders and spread out to block off any escape.

Most of the disciples had dozed off by the time the captain raised his arm to signal his men to halt. Judas walked up to Yeshua, addressing him as Rabbi. He greeted him as usual with a kiss. Immediately a detail of soldiers stepped forward, torches flickering in the dark and weapons at the ready. The air was cool and a faint breeze ruffled Yeshua's beard.

He stepped towards the approaching soldiers and calmly asked them who they were looking for.

The captain replied gruffly. 'Which one of you is Yeshua the Nazarene?'

Yeshua who by now was illuminated by the torches threw back his hood and said in a loud voice, 'I am!'

The image of Yeshua glowing in the light of the torches and his bold reply of 'I am', a term better known as one of the names of G_d himself, frightened the soldiers and they fell back, stumbling over one another in the dark. Many had witnessed his teaching in the Temple and secretly feared him. Would he turn his miraculous powers in divine revenge against them?

In the confusion, Peter drew a sword he had concealed under his cloak and lunged at one of the slaves of the High Priest. Yeshua reprimanded him. He wanted nothing to do with violence.

Judas, on the other hand, had been encouraged by Yeshua's reply and took further comfort by his apparent defence of the arresting party. It was if he wanted to be arrested, so he was not alarmed when the captain's men took hold of him and bound his hands and led him away. The disciples ran for their lives, but some followed the guard at a safe distance all the way back to Caiaphas' house and into the outer courtyard of the courtroom.

Caiaphas had used the time to summon as many members of the Council as he could for an initial interrogation. Among them were former High Priests, Pharisees, and senior members of the Council. Judas and Simon followed them into the chamber, standing at the back near the door.

Simon urged Judas to leave with him, since his work was done, but he was adamant he wanted to stay and watch. He was still fully expecting a change of scene and for Yeshua to be hailed as Messiah before being taken to the Temple and anointed King.

What he then saw was something very different. Simon stood nervously to one side. In truth he had simply failed to consider what would happen to Judas as he faced his own betrayal. He had been so preoccupied with getting to this point and dealing with the threat to himself that he had simply overlooked what would happen as a consequence. But now everything was about to unravel with alarming speed.

Judas became more agitated, and Simon tried again to get him out of the courtroom but to no avail. He began to think about how to deal with the impending situation.

Yeshua was standing in the centre of the chamber, his hands still tied behind his back. The questioning began and he just stood there and said nothing. None of the questioners were able to corroborate their evidence accurately, with witness after witness contradicting each other.

Judas looked appalled and confused. His face said it all. Again, Simon attempted to get him to leave, but Judas just stood there transfixed.

Finally, Caiaphas, who had been listening to the pathetic and chaotic questioning, which was producing no response in Yeshua at all, stepped forward. Yeshua just stood there staring straight ahead, silently enduring the onslaught of accusations with a wall of silence. He walked up to him face to face and began to speak to him calmly. The change of mood spread throughout the courtroom. Yeshua continued to stare straight ahead.

'What do you make of all these questions then?' Yeshua made no answer. 'Do you have no defence? Is that it? Perhaps you're not the Messiah after all?' After a brief pause, he continued. 'You really don't have an answer, do you? Nothing to say to your accusers?' he moved closer and spoke directly into his face. 'You're just a big fake, aren't you? Just a load of hot air. Is that it?

'Let me put it to you directly. Are you the Messiah, the son of the Blessed One?' He waited for a response his anger boiling inside and just below the surface.

Yeshua lowered his distant gaze, looking Caiaphas straight in the eye. Very calmly and quietly, he replied, 'I am.' There was a sharp intake of breath from all around. These were the sacred words of the great I AM, the name of G_d Almighty. The entire assembly was aghast.

Yeshua went on. 'And what's more, you will see the Son of Man sitting at the right hand of power and coming with the clouds of heaven.'

Judas' heart skipped a beat. Was this the moment he had been waiting for?

As for all the others, utter mayhem broke loose. The High Priest took hold of his sacred priestly garments and with all the strength he could muster unleashed a blood curdling cry as he tore the fabric apart. People covered their ears, screaming to keep the blasphemy out. The noise was deafening and the uproar a frenzy.

'We don't need any more witness statements!' bellowed Caiaphas triumphantly. 'You've heard it straight from his own mouth!' His face was so red it looked as if he was going to explode. Saliva was spilling from either side of his enraged mouth and dribbling down his beard. He called for quiet. 'You've all heard the blasphemy for yourselves. So what's your verdict?' He was so out of breath he could hardly get the words out. He was in such a rage.

With one accord they all condemned Yeshua as deserving death.

All the pent-up anger and fury poured out at Yeshua. People were shouting at him and abusing him, accusing him of blasphemy, blindfolding him and then striking him and ridiculing him. They taunted him to prophesy who had hit him.

Yeshua made no defence as the blows rained down on him.

Judas turned to Simon. 'What have I done?' he gasped. 'What have I done?'

Simon said nothing.

The High Priest collected himself and turned to leave. He realised that there was yet more work to do to secure the death penalty, which only the Roman authorities could administer.

Judas lunged forward. He tried to grab hold of the High Priest, but Simon restrained him. 'You promised to anoint Yeshua as King, but you've tricked me!' he shouted above the din. 'You made a promise to me and my uncle you would do it!' he repeated, realising he was in a courtroom and drawing Simon in as his witness.

Caiaphas stopped. 'Your uncle?' Your uncle?' he snarled derisively. He drew up so close to Judas that he could smell his foul breath. 'He's not your uncle, you miserable little creature! He's your father! Yes, your father!'

Judas looked at Simon for reassurance. There was none. Simon's head hung low, saying it all. 'My father?' he questioned.

'Tell him the truth Simon! Go on, tell him!' snapped Caiaphas with relish and then turning the witness point around which had irked him he added, 'We both know the truth, Simon, don't we? You failed to deliver the evidence I paid you for and this little bastard held out!

'This trial would have been a lot easier if you had done your job!

'What job? What are you talking about?' demanded Judas.

'Tell him, Simon!'

Simon remained silent.

'Tell him how you agreed to take down the evidence for me about Yeshua and use, yes *use* your own son to get access!' Caiaphas glanced at Judas. 'Tell him, Simon!' he demanded again.

Finally, Simon spoke. He tried to explain his way out of it, but it only made matters worse.

'Is this true? Are you...are you...my father?' asked Judas, barely able to comprehend the situation.

'Yes, it's true,' said Simon finally admitting it. 'But it all happened a long time ago.'

But Judas had no heart to hear the detail. He recalled a conversation he had overheard between his mother and his grandmother long ago. He was in the next room, and they were arguing but didn't know Judas was listening. His grandmother had let slip that he was a bastard. He didn't fully understand at the time, but now he did.

'You raped my mother, didn't you? And then you tricked your own son to betray Yeshua, knowing all the time what would happen to him! Oh my... Oh my...' his voice tailed off as he covered his face in shame.

Caiaphas, seeing his dirty work was done, pushed past Judas who had been blocking the doorway. 'I've got work to do.' he said as he strode off down the corridor. No one would hear any nasty rumours from Judas now, he thought. He left Simon to pick up the pieces.

Simon tried to justify himself. 'It wasn't like that, I can explain...' but Judas had heard enough, and he spun around and ran out of the Chamber.

He just ran and ran. He saw the Temple and, not knowing where to go or what to do, he ran up the steps into the Temple area looking for help. He kept going, entering the restricted areas. There was no one about since most of the Temple Guards had been involved in the arrest. He stopped to think, but all he could think about was the awful truth which he would have to live with for the rest of his life. That he had betrayed Yeshua for money! His mind was racing. To think his own father had deliberately misled him. How could anyone trick their own son, yes, their own son, into doing such a thing?

Tears welled up in his eyes. The realization was just too hard to bear. He fumbled in his pocket and brought out the leather bag of coins. Thirty pieces of silver. He opened the bag and as he walked forward, he tipped out the contents into his hand. He threw the money as hard as he could across the floor of the sanctuary. The silver coins rang out as they scattered across the stone floor.

The noise alerted a guard who immediately appeared with an official and reprimanded him for being there, but he didn't care.

'I've sinned by betraying innocent blood,' he told them.

'That's your business. Deal with it,' he replied and promptly escorted him out into the night.

Outside he began to walk. He was sobbing uncontrollably, and he just kept walking, not knowing where he was going and overcome with remorse.

He walked aimlessly down towards the Kidron valley where Yeshua would have gone to reach the garden at Gethsemane. Once outside he just kept walking. Eventually he came across a goat tied to a tree by a short length of rope. It had used up all the available grass and didn't seem to have anything to drink. He felt sorry for it. He could identify with it so he untied it and let it go. Now it was free. As it wandered off into the night and freedom it made him even sadder. There was no freedom for Judas and there never would be.

He looked up at the tree. There was a bough reaching out over a drop in the landscape. He took the end of the rope and made a noose. He climbed up and sat on the branch looking out towards the city. 'If only Yeshua were here,' he thought, 'perhaps he would understand.' He had only done what he thought was right, but how wrong he had been. He loved Yeshua, who had chosen him as a disciple, even one of the twelve. He had followed him. Surely he would understand? But now, who knows where he was; in a dungeon somewhere, and it was all his fault.

He thought about his mother, her gentle hands and her warm embrace. He thought about his childhood and Uncle Simon... his father. He loved them all but he felt utterly betrayed, and yet he was the betrayer. It was unbearable; irreconcilable. The more he thought about it, the more he went round and round in circles. What a mess! There was no way out.

Tears continued to roll down his face. He could see very little through the tears and through the darkness. He called out to G_d but there was no reply, only silence. He felt utterly, utterly alone.

He tied the rope around the branch and slipped the noose over his head and just sat there sobbing.

Then, very slowly, he pitched forward, and in a moment he felt himself falling.

As he fell it was as if time stood still.

He felt incredibly sorry about everything. About what he had done, even who he was. His stupid obsession with money. Everything about his miserable life.

Who can tell what happens between a person and their G_d in such moments; such very small moments...

Then everything went still.

There was no more to remember; no more pain; no more to think; finally; eternally, no more.

Yet somewhere across the city and alone in the darkness of a dungeon, a man wept and wept and wept.

# PART 3

# ON THE RUN

*"While I thought that I was learning how to live,
I have been learning how to die."*
Leonardo da Vinci

Chapter 17

# ESCAPE FROM JERUSALEM

Simon had been up all night looking for Judas but there was no sign of him anywhere. He learnt that he had been seen last in the Temple but after that the trail went cold.

Hungry, tired, and dejected he made his way back to his apartment. Wearily he climbed up the stone steps and walked slowly down the corridor to his rooms.

Inside he sat down at his table. Dawn was not far away, and he didn't feel like sleep.

He got up and went through to his bedroom, kneeling down by the alcove. He lifted the skirting board to gain access to the underfloor hiding place and reached down beneath the floorboards to retrieve the leather carry case containing the scrolls.

He returned to the table and was about to open the case when suddenly he heard voices and then footsteps in the corridor.

'His is the last room on the left.' He recognised Anna's voice.

There was not a second to lose. He grabbed the case and squeezed into the small alcove behind the door where he normally hung his cloak, and only just in time.

The door swung open flattening his head between the wooden coat pegs. Two armed guards burst in violently. His heart was pounding while the two of them made a detailed search of his flat. They went through everything throwing his clothes, his papers, and all his personal effects on the floor.

Then they entered his sleeping area.

'Hey, look at this!' shouted one of the guards, kneeling down by the alcove. With the secret floorboard displaced, it was easy to see that the compartment was empty.

'Looks as if we missed him,' observed the second guard, looking over the shoulder of the first.

Anna was still standing by the door.

'He was here a short while ago, I saw him come in.'

'Well, he's not here now, is he?' one of the guards replied sarcastically. 'There's nothing here.'

The two men made a final check of the apartment before they left. There was a small crack in the door and Simon could see the face of one of the guards standing in front of the door, lamp in hand. His heart was in his mouth. Surely he would be discovered at any moment.

'You wouldn't know where he's hiding, would you?' The guard took hold of Anna's arm firmly. 'It wouldn't do to be hiding him, would it?' he added menacingly.

'No, I swear to G_d, I'm just the maid here. I've no idea where he is. He never discusses his business with me. Like I said, he was here a minute ago.' They could see she was frightened and not hiding anything.

The two men pushed past her and left abruptly, taking the lamp with them and leaving Anna in the dark. She followed at a safe distance feeling her way down the corridor and back down the stairs.

Simon eased out of his hiding place. He had been lucky this time and he needed to get out of Jerusalem as fast as possible. He stuffed some things into his travelling bag and then reached down into the recess below the floor. On a discreet shelf, tucked up out of sight, was a small bag of coins. He quietly retrieved it, creeping out into the dark corridor, taking care not to tread on the creaky boards.

He got as far as the door, but someone appeared in the lobby. It startled him. It was Anna. She looked up at him thinking that he was just coming in.

'There were two men here a minute ago looking for you. I had to let them in, and they've made a terrible mess in your room, but I'll give you a hand to clear it up if you like.'

'No, that won't be necessary, Anna. If I'm quick I can catch them up and then we can see what they want, can't we?' And with that he darted out of the door without even saying goodbye and disappeared into the street.

Now that he knew Caiaphas was after him, his immediate focus was to avoid arrest. He planned to head north before turning west, but his first problem was to find a change of clothes. He was still dressed like a Scribe in full white robes.

He raised his hood and turned up a back street where he knew there was a trader who dealt in second-hand clothes. He had often bought things from him in the past, but no sooner had he done so than he spotted the two guards ahead of him, talking to each other. He darted back out of sight.

Now what would he do? While he was trying to think of a solution, who should appear around the corner but the clothes dealer. He recognised Simon immediately.

Simon greeted him warmly hardly believing his luck.

'What brings you out at this hour, sir?' he enquired.

'I was just on my way to pay you a visit,' Simon said feebly, aware of the early hour, 'I was hoping to purchase some clothing.'

'It's a bit early to be open for business right now, Sir. You're lucky to catch me, I got word that there was to be a crucifixion and I'm just on my way there now. Not that I'm into crucifixions, you understand, it's just that sometimes I can buy a bit of stock off the soldiers at a good price, if you know what I mean.' The trader looked a bit awkward, aware that buying the clothes off dead convicts didn't sound a brilliant way of promoting his business.

'Oh,' said Simon fumbling with his money purse, 'that's a pity. I could make it worth your while if you know what *I* mean?'

The trader looked at his white clothes. 'Not sure I've got much in your style right now, I'm afraid. What were you after?'

Simon took a deep breath not wanting to give too much away. 'I was hoping to buy some *ordinary* clothes; I'm going away to stay with a friend. Sort of off duty; you know.'

It sounded unlikely, but he had been paid a visit earlier by the two guards and was smart enough not to ask any questions if there was a good deal to be had.

'Better come this way,' he said, guiding Simon towards a back street. 'I have a back entrance to the shop,' he added discreetly.

A short while later the two men emerged from the shop with Simon dressed very ordinarily, but definitely not cheaply. It occurred to him that he might use his new travelling companion as a useful cover to get out of the city.

'Mind if I walk with you?' asked Simon.

'If you like. I'm going to the Praetorium first. I know one of the soldiers on the gate. Quiet word; you know,' he added knowingly.

The two men walked up to the Roman headquarters, hoods up, in silence. Simon's new disguise had been a huge stroke of good fortune, particularly when they walked straight past two more Temple guards without being recognised.

'That was lucky,' remarked the trader once past.

'Luck or something else,' remarked Simon, aware that his good fortune might be more than coincidental.

They pushed their way through the gathering crowd towards the gate of the Praetorium, where two soldiers were standing guard. The trader spoke briefly to one of them. Simon waited at the corner of the wall. There was quite a noise coming from inside, but through the gap between the wall and the wooden gate post he could just make out a figure being scourged, tied to a post in the courtyard. As he swayed to and fro under the flails of his two tormentors, his face turned, and Simon immediately realised it was Yeshua. He was shocked by what he saw. His face was almost unrecognisable, swollen and bloodied. His back was stripped bare and bleeding profusely under the repetitive strokes of the notorious barbed Roman flagrum, the welts extending right around his body.

The noise was coming from the soldiers. Simon could see one of the soldiers carrying out the punishment standing legs astride, scourge in one hand, pausing for breath under the exertion, wiping his blood-spattered face. The others, who had bets on whether the prisoner would stay standing or pass out under the punishment, were urging him on. There was no love between the 10th Legion and a Jew.

Eventually, the ordeal was over, and the winning punters let out a roar of triumph.

They untied Yeshua and dragged him off out of view. The other side of the Praetorium led out onto a small square with an elevated stone seat known as the Pavement. Judging by the noise, the square was full of people. The Governor, Pontius Pilate, crossed over the courtyard to take up his place at the judgement seat.

Simon could hear voices heckling the Governor but couldn't tell what was being said until he heard a crescendo of cries calling out in repetitive unison. 'Crucify him!'

Simon had learnt from the trader that among the crucifixions arranged for that morning was the leader of a Jewish terrorist group called Yeshua Barabba, who specialised in staging riots and then, under cover of the ensuing confusion, the group would attack and kill the Roman soldiers sent to deal with it. His luck had run out, however, and he had been caught and convicted.

It was a tradition at Passover for the Roman Governor to release and pardon one prisoner as a gesture of good will.

Pilate had been told about the popularity of Yeshua and had calculated that if he offered to pardon Yeshua his offer would be accepted. He had been concerned that the Jewish terrorist Yeshua Barabba would be released. Unfortunately, Pilate badly miscalculated and the people immediately demanded that Barabba be released.

Coincidentally the name Yeshua Barabba meant 'Saviour, Son of the father'. So as dawn broke over Jerusalem that day, in a strange twist, Yeshua (Saviour) of Nazareth, Son of The Father, was committed for crucifixion and would effectively die in the place of Yeshua (saviour) son of the father (Barabba).

The decision did not go down at all well with the Praetorium guard, who were relishing the opportunity of exacting revenge for the loss of their comrades. The mood in the courtyard was not pleasant.

Yeshua was brought back into the courtyard. Soon a menacing group of soldiers surrounded him. Just then the centurion emerged from the building with the charge board to be nailed to Yeshua's cross.

'What's the charge, eh?' called out one of the soldiers.

'It says here that he's The King of the Jews!' he read it out slowly. The soldiers roared with derisory laughter.

'A king needs royal treatment!' taunted another.

With one eye looking through the gap by the corner post of the gate, Simon could just make out what was going on. They were literally playing with Yeshua, pushing him around and mocking him. Many of these soldiers were recruits from the Syro Phoenician area of the region and were intensely antisemitic.

Then another soldier produced a majestic looking cloak, which they threw over him, 'making sure it fit' by pressing it roughly onto his back. Yeshua winced with pain. Soon they had all joined in.

One drew his sword and hacked off a couple of branches from a nearby thorn bush and with his thick leather gloves, twisted them together in the shape of a crown. He rammed it firmly onto Yeshua's head. The pain was intense, and blood began to pour out of his torn scalp. He involuntarily tried to lift it off, but the thorns were stuck fast like barbs. There was more mocking laughter.

One soldier produced a swagger stick made of a reed.

'A king needs a sceptre to rule with! Now we have a proper little king, don't we?' he snarled and thrust the reed into Yeshua's hand, but he dropped it on the ground.

'Don't want to rule any more, do we?' He bent down and, picking up the reed, began beating him over the head in a frenzy of anger. This caused further pain by jabbing the thorns into his head with every stroke.

Just then the centurion returned.

'Let's be getting this prisoner ready for execution!' he barked and immediately the men set about wrenching off the crown of thorns. Yeshua cried out in pain and knelt there with his head in his hands nursing the intense pain. They tore off the robe and dragged him to his feet, making him put his clothes back on, ready for departure. Meanwhile the other soldiers tied a *patibulum* across his shoulders– a wooden plank on which he would be crucified.

Simon watched in horror. He had never witnessed such treatment and it frightened him. He thought about making his get-away out of Jerusalem, but something held him back. He couldn't bear to watch and yet he couldn't tear himself away.

'Fetch the other prisoners and bring 'em up 'ere!' ordered the centurion.

Three men were crouching in darkness in a cell below ground, listening to the torture and awaiting their fate. They were dragged out into the yard, terrified, squinting in the bright light. They were crying out for mercy, hands tied behind them.

The centurion stepped forward and grabbed Barabba by the hair and stood him to one side.

'Prepare the prisoners for execution!'

The two remaining prisoners were prepared by laying a *patibulum* across their shoulders and tying back their arms.

'Open the gates!' shouted the centurion. 'You're free to go!' The centurion thrust Barabba towards the open gate. He just stood there, afraid to run, fearing a trap. He looked at Yeshua, bloodied and bruised.

'Who, me?' he questioned.

'Yes, you! Now get out of my sight before I re-arrest you!' shouted the centurion.

Simon stood at the edge of the open gate behind the guard. He watched Barabba take one look at the crucifixion detail, who were glaring menacingly at him, and begin to move slowly toward the gate. Suddenly he broke into a terrified sprint like a wild animal released from a cage. And then he disappeared into the crowd.

'Detail, forward march!' The centurion ordered his grizzly procession out of the Praetorium into the street. A sizeable crowd had gathered to witness the spectacle as they headed towards the city gates. People strained to get a better view of the prisoners, but the one they had come to see most was not there. Instead, it was the Miracle Man from Nazareth.

What they saw took them by surprise. Of this mortal cortege of three, one of the prisoners looked half dead already. Blood spattered, the man struggled to carry his *patibulum*. This thick plank of wood was a little wider than an arms' span, but it was heavy and he was struggling under the load. Lagging behind already, the soldiers bullied and beat him to catch up.

Yeshua, weakened by his ordeal and still in shock, was clearly not going to make it on his own.

Simon followed at a safe distance, being careful not to be recognised. The weather was overcast and there was a chill in the air, and he was glad to be wearing his new outfit, which was more suited to cold and wet weather than his traditional clothing. The cloak had a large hood and there was good reason to have it up, which was a comfort. Compared to the spectacle he was now watching, his 'comfort' seemed shamefully out of place despite his own danger.

The procession had not gone very far when there was a loud gasp from the crowd followed by an outburst of orders in Latin. Simon just caught a glimpse of Yeshua lying face down in the street, the beam lying across the back of his head. He lay motionless for a moment or two. With no way of protecting his fall he had hit the stone paving face first, with the heavy beam propelling him forward and pinning him to the ground with a sickening thud.

Despite the shouts and lashes of the soldiers he lay motionless on the ground, unconscious.

The centurion, who was bringing up the rear, stepped forward.

'You stupid idiots! There'll be no prizes for crucifying a dead man! Get that beam off him now!'

As the soldiers untied him, Yeshua slowly regained consciousness. He tried to get back up on his feet but lost his balance and was about to fall again when the centurion caught him. He lowered him to the ground where he sat dazed at his feet.

The centurion looked around.

'Oi! You!' he pointed to a man on the edge of the crowd. Simon from Cyrene stood there terrified. His wife grabbed his arm. They had come out early to buy some provisions for the festival and were making their way back to their lodgings.

'Get over here now and carry this crossbeam!' Simon and his wife stood rooted to the ground.

'I said *now!*' bawled the Centurion unused to having his orders ignored.

Simon of Cyrene stepped forward slowly, his wife watching in horror. He looked down pitifully at the prisoner. Yeshua looked up at him. Even through the bruising and swelling of his face he could see this was no ordinary criminal. Nothing was said, but Simon felt a sense of identity with this man. It wasn't just pity that he felt rising up, it was something else that he didn't recognise. It was a feeling of compassion, and it made Simon feel angry. The boldness that followed took him by surprise.

Despite his kindly appearance Simon was strongly built but this rising anger filled his body with new strength. He stooped down and effortlessly picked up the heavy plank as if it was half the weight and put it over his right shoulder. He didn't mind that it was covered in blood. With a smile he offered his free hand to Yeshua and helped him to his feet.

The procession continued slowly, with Simon of Cyrene following Yeshua, who periodically looked back as if to check he was alright. People lined the narrow streets on either side and followed as the tortuous route took them out through the city gates and up to *Gol'gotha*, the place of execution. The Romans had especially chosen this site not only for its position next to one of the busiest roads in and out of Jerusalem, giving it maximum exposure, but also because of a gruesome image in the hillside rock formation that closely resembled a skull.

The sight of this image said it all. As the procession approached, it had the effect of striking fear into the very souls of those following. The low murmurs of the crowd began to take on a more menacing tone and jibes of derision could be heard instead. It was as if the fear induced an angry reaction in them. They also knew what was coming next.

On this day, many had turned out in support of Yeshua Barabba. He was a popular figure, a symbol of Jewish resistance against the hated Romans. He had struck a blow for freedom and fought back against Pontius Pilate, the ruling Prefect whose sadistic methods of law enforcement had drawn criticism even from the Emperor Tiberius himself. So, as news of his release filtered through Jerusalem, a mood of rejoicing had followed.

Now they wanted to see what would happen to the miracle man from Nazareth who had taken his place. Rumours abounded about what he might do. Might he miraculously start a revolution resulting in the overthrow of the Romans? Was he the long-awaited Messiah, the Anointed One, who would lead them all out of Roman slavery? Some were there to find out.

Others were there because they were his supporters from Galilee, drawn to Jerusalem for Passover. They wanted to be there for very different reasons.

For Simon Ish Kerioth, there was no good reason to be there. If he had any sense, he would be putting as much distance between himself and Jerusalem as he could, but there was something drawing him which, despite his great intellect, he didn't understand. A large part of him was convinced Yeshua was not the Messiah, but there was another part, a growing part, that was not so sure.

Finally, they reached *Gol'gotha*, the Place of the Skull, also known as Calvary or *Calvariæ Locus* to the Romans.

There stood several blood-stained upright stakes made from olive wood, with short wooden pegs driven into each stake, marking the place of torture. On this occasion three would be used.

As the prisoners approached, two of their number began desperately pleading for mercy, but today there would be no mercy. The other stood wearily but impassively awaiting his ordeal.

The clothes dealer watched from a distance as the first prisoner was untied from his *patibulum* and stripped naked, his garments tossed onto the ground. Two soldiers either side held him by the wrists as they wrestled him down on top of the beam, shouting abuse at him and stretching out his arms. A third stood by with a handful of large rough headed nails and a lump hammer. He knelt down and quickly drove a nail through the man's arm just above the wrist, impaling him to the wooden crossbeam, before repeating the procedure on the other side.

The tortured screams and agonising contortions that followed silenced the crowd.

There was worse to come. The prisoner was dragged to his feet and the crossbeam was hauled up the upright stake and secured at the top. His full weight was supported at first by his feet on the ground, but then he was lifted onto the thick seat peg known as a *sedile* jutting out of the stake. This was designed to induce further pain while at the same time prolonging the agony by giving just enough support to his body. Finally, his legs were twisted sideways and drawn up into a tortuous sideways crouching position before a large nail was driven through both feet, entering from the outside of the ankle. The screaming prisoner squirmed and twisted under the excruciating pain. [1]

No one watching could be in any doubt that this was not just a means of execution but a cruel method of torture by deliberately prolonging death. Furthermore, the public spectacle was designed as a strong incentive to stay out of trouble.

The whole process was carried out with military precision and speed.

Now it was Yeshua's turn.

Simon of Cyrene had been ordered to drop the crossbeam at the foot of the next stake and then dismissed. He returned to his wife, who had followed the procession and was standing nervously at the edge of the crowd. Together they watched in horror as Yeshua was pushed to the ground and the whole ghastly process was repeated before their eyes, only there was a difference.

As the young soldiers took hold of his hands, he did not resist their grip. The soldier had no idea whose hand he was holding, but for Yeshua it would be the last time he would feel the hand of another person. He turned his head and looked down his arm at the soldier.

'Father, forgive them, because they don't know what they are doing.'

His words were clearly audible to the hushed crowd and the young soldier looked up at him briefly. It was just a glimpse, but that picture of a man he didn't know looking at him forgivingly would remain with him for the rest of his life. Instead of fear and hatred, there was something else looking at him. It was as if the prisoner was interested in him. He seemed to be enquiring into him. What was that? He was well used to the job, in fact he prided himself at doing it well, but this was something he hadn't come across before.

Then the first nail struck home, and the cry of pain was just like any other. The soldier dismissed his thoughts, but they would return to him later, again and again, in the years to come.

While the soldiers went about their business, a group of others stood guard in line between them and the crowd.

Mary, Yeshua's mother, was among the crowd, and from where she was standing, she could see her son visible between the soldier's legs, lying on the ground. As the first nail was driven home, she instinctively turned away. She desperately wanted to leave but she instinctively wanted to be there with him.

John, Yeshua's cousin and close disciple, and the women who had come to support Mary were standing alongside and tried to comfort her. She could see the High Priests, Caiaphas and Annas, with some Pharisees and scribes. There were others there whom she knew personally. She felt anger and disgust that they had turned out to witness her son being tortured this way, particularly as they had been the principal instigators.

What could she do? She felt powerless and she cried out to G_d to do something to stop it all, but today G_d was silent. She had heard her son's prayer of forgiveness, but she found it hard to understand him saying such a thing. She felt no forgiveness at all. How could she? It would take a while before she would be in a place to imitate her son.

To the other side of her, and unseen, was another man. His head was covered, and he was standing back from the front of the crowd, close enough to see but far enough away not to be recognised. He was Simon Ish Kerioth. From where he was standing, he could see Peter and some of the other disciples. They too were making themselves as much a part of the crowd as they could. These were dangerous times. Their leader was being crucified and if they weren't careful, they could be next.

By 9am all three prisoners were impaled on their crosses.

Some soldiers stood guard, while others gathered up the last possessions of the crucified men and began to share them out among each other. Yeshua had been wearing a beautifully made tunic woven in one piece and they decided to gamble for it. It had been given to Yeshua as a gift. How could they know what priceless healing power had flowed through the hem alone? Little did the clothes dealer know what its true value might be.

Meanwhile, the crowd were beginning to get restless. The occasional taunt had gained momentum and it was all too clear which of the prisoners they were taunting. But it wasn't just the nature of the taunts that was remarkable, it was the people who were doing the taunting that frightened his supporters. For them personally it was hurtful, insulting, and senseless. But to hear those in power and authority behaving like rabble-rousers against a man they had successfully persuaded the Romans to crucify meant that the position of being his disciple was not a good place to be.

Simon Ish Kerioth knew all too well how these people could turn on their adversaries, and this was a clear signal to make himself scarce and not to risk being recognised. But he still felt compelled to stay. Working alongside this strange man for so long had taught him that you could never tell what would happen next. He noticed that even one of the prisoners being crucified alongside him was hurling abuse at him. Why was everyone so against this man who had done so much good?

For three hours the crowd hung around, attracted by a ghoulish magnetism. What were they waiting for? Were they half expecting some sort of divine deliverance? If so, why the loathing and taunting?

Then at noon the weather began to deteriorate. It had been overcast and damp, but that was all about to change. The sky turned darker and darker until it was like nightfall. As time passed, and sensing rain, people began to drift away. Then, as the crowd dispersed, the rain began to fall, gently at first but then slowly turning into a heavy downpour, and what had begun as a fairly orderly dispersal turned into chaos. People were slipping and sliding in the mud under a deluge of rain. They were pushing and shoving one another as they tried to maintain balance and get back to the city for cover.

For the prisoners on their crosses and the soldiers there was no relief.

Yeshua had been trying to maintain consciousness. The trickle of rain down his swollen face and body washed over his wounds. He drew himself up against the nails and looked across towards the Temple.

The people who had remained behind were largely supporters.

As time went on Simon drew a little closer, emboldened by the absence of authority figures, most of whom he knew. With his hood firmly up against both recognition and now the rain, he looked at Yeshua impaled on the cross.

Yeshua turned his head and looked down at Simon. He half opened his mouth to speak but nothing came out. His mouth was dry and rough like a shard from an old earthenware pot. His tongue stuck to the roof of his mouth. His body was twisted sideways, and he was obviously in a lot of skeletal pain. He was trying to speak, but Simon couldn't make out what he was saying. Yeshua began again but the frustration was very evident on his face. He coughed to clear his lungs, which were slowly filling with fluid. The resulting mouthful helped.

A man nearby thought he was calling on Elijah, so the centurion took a sponge which was in a cup of sour wine and with the aid of a spear, lifted it to his lips. Yeshua took some and rinsed out his mouth.

He drew himself up and with a supreme effort bellowed out what he had been trying to say.

This time Simon got it. He wasn't talking about Elijah, it was the first verse of Psalm 22, the self-same psalm which Simon had been copying out barely a week before. Every word was fresh in his mind and Yeshua was speaking out the words of the first verse.

'Eloi, Eloi…

'My G_d, my G_d, why have you forsaken me…' Yeshua's voice tailed off.

Simon always understood this to be a Psalm of David, the great king of Israel. It spoke of David's suffering but here in front of Simon, Yeshua was taking it for his own.

As Simon recited the psalm under his breath, he realised that what he was looking at was exactly what David had described. It spoke of David's tongue cleaving to the roof of his mouth, in fact it spoke of all the horrible things he was now seeing in front of him.

Yeshua was watching Simon as he recited the rest of the Psalm under his breath.

'But I am a worm and not a man, scorned and despised by every-one. All who see me mock me; they hurl insults, shaking their heads.

"He trusts in the Lord," they scoff, "Let the Lord rescue him! Let him deliver him since he delights in him!"

'Yet you brought me out of my mother's womb and you made me trust in you from the time I suckled at her breast with my very first mouthful of milk. You have been my G_d from the very beginning.

'Stay close to me for trouble is near and I have no one else to turn to. The bulls and lions of hell are circling around me waiting for the chance to eat me.

'I am poured out like water and all my bones are out of joint. My heart has turned to melted wax. My mouth is as dry as a shard and my tongue sticks to the roof of my mouth. It feels as if I'm lying in the dust of death itself.

'I am surrounded by a pack of dogs. Pierced through, hand and foot, every part of me on display for all to stare and gloat over. They even gamble for my clothes.

'But you, my Lord, please don't leave me! Quick Lord! You're all I have left. Don't let me be eaten by these dogs and lions or impaled on the horns of these evil beasts.'

Suddenly, Simon stopped mouthing the words. Yeshua was still looking at him. And then the truth hit him. This was David, the suffering servant. The King of the Jews. He read the charge written on the board over his head. Here was the Son of David, just like they said of him; the Netzer, the tender green shoot; Yeshua the Nazarene.

Simon was overwhelmed by an intense sensation of being abandoned by his G_d – the G_d of Israel – it was he, Simon Ish Kerioth, who also felt forsaken, alone and abandoned, and yet here was The Suffering Servant, the true Suffering Servant, abandoned with him. Feeling that self-same forsaken feeling. Not looking down from on high but looking down from a cross! Taking it all upon himself; everything Simon had ever felt about himself – Yeshua had taken it upon himself.

The thought was overwhelming.

'So this is what it's all about!' he mumbled, the tears welling up in his eyes. His chest began to heave with involuntary sobs. He just stood there looking at Yeshua. He felt he was probably the only person there who had fully understood what Yeshua had cried out in his pain and anguish.

As all this dawned on Simon, he thought he saw the faintest glimpse of a smile on the swollen lips of Yeshua. Even through all the swelling and bruising that disfigured his tortured face, a faint smile was nevertheless still visible.

A thought occurred to him as he stood there. He slipped a hand beneath his cloak and touched the leather carry case containing the scrolls. A notion ran through his mind.

'If this man is who I think he is, the Messiah, then these scrolls in my possession are no longer the evidence against him, they are instead words of eternal life!'

The self-same words Simon had carefully recorded as evidence for the prosecution had just become the principal evidence for the defence. Then suddenly he snapped back to the frightening reality of where he was and who was trying to arrest him. If that happened there would be no hope for these words. They would almost certainly be destroyed.

He realised he must get away at all costs. He turned to leave, and his heart froze. There, not twenty paces away, were two Temple guards with their backs to him. But behind them were six others looking straight at him. He quickly turned back to Yeshua, who was straining to lift himself up, but before he could do anything he heard the words he had been dreading.

144

'Halt! In the name of the High Priest!' shouted their commander. What would he do now? It was too late to run, and he couldn't outrun them anyway. The two guards nearest him advanced towards him at speed.

At that very second Yeshua let out a bloodcurdling cry. Simon didn't quite catch what he said, but as he slumped down you could hear his bones crack as the full weight of his body tore against the nails. He slipped off the peg supporting his weight and pitched forward, his head lolling and his tongue just protruding between his swollen lips. A feint gurgling sound ensued as his last breath wheezed out.

Everyone had frozen still at this sudden event, including the guards. The centurion, who was standing a few feet away from Simon, looked up at Yeshua and murmured just loud enough for Simon to hear, 'Surely this man was Son of G_d!'

Simon looked at the centurion and then back at the guards, who were slithering across the mud, desperate to arrest him.

Simon wasted no time. He circled around in front of the centurion, placing the Roman between his pursuers and himself. But it was a futile move. The centurion alarmed at Simon being between him and the prisoners immediately drew his sword and lunged forward in pursuit. Heavily weighed down by his armour, he lost his balance and slipped over, falling forward and impeding the advance of the guards.

Arrest seemed inevitable. The situation was hopeless. But then something extraordinary happened. The ground, which was already extremely slippery began to move. In fact, it moved so violently that Simon also nearly fell over.

The three crosses rocked back and forth, causing the two other prisoners to cry out in pain. Yeshua made no sound. He was already dead.

Simon had the advantage of being on the opposite side of a slight incline and launched himself off down the slope while the guards struggled to get to the summit.

Meanwhile panic had broken out and people were trying to get away towards the city gates as quickly as possible. This played into Simon's hands. He was enveloped in the retreating crowd and in the confusion, he managed to get a head start on the guards, who had lost sight of him and assumed he had headed back to the city with everyone else.

In fact, in the chaos he managed to turn off the approach to Jerusalem along a narrow track that ran beside the city wall before heading north. He kept going for nearly a mile before he stopped to look back and, to his relief, saw no sign of his pursuers. It was still raining hard, and he was soaked through to the skin.

It was now past three o'clock in the afternoon and there was little chance of reaching the inn where he had originally planned to spend the night. Sundown, when the Passover Sabbath began, would make it impossible to find accommodation. The guards, meanwhile, had returned to Jerusalem and were conducting a fruitless search, giving Simon a head start as they too would be confined to barracks following sundown.

But he needed somewhere to stay for the night. It was then that he remembered a notorious hostel that no one in their right mind would stay at. It was a dreadful place full of fleas, bedbugs, and drunks. The good thing about it was that it was within reach, even if a little off the beaten track. It was also a place where it was unlikely he would be recognised!

He would stay there, G_d preserve him, until the Passover and Sabbath were over. Then he would set off, despite the risk of travelling after dark, and head west for a destination he had in mind where it would be unlikely he would be found. Hopefully in time the search party would discover where he had stayed and assume he was heading north.

By the time he reached the hostel the rain had eased, and evening was closing in. The hostel innkeeper would be getting ready to eat the traditional *Seder* with his family and any others staying there to celebrate Passover, as it was 14th of Nissan.

Before he decided what to do, he had a brief look around the back to see if he could find any shelter where he could sleep for the night. There was a small group of outbuildings about twenty yards from the house and behind one he found a log store under a lean-to. The wood was dry, and the overhanging roof would keep the elements off him. It wasn't the most comfortable bed, but it was somewhere to sleep. He was tired and hungry, and he wasn't expecting to sleep that well anyway.

Using his travelling bag as a pillow, he curled up as best he could against the shed wall, wrapping his sodden cloak around him. The leather scroll case had fared well in the rain and was pretty dry. Fortunately, it was a mild night and he managed to snatch some sleep, albeit waking frequently.

His dreams were gruesome; filled with ghastly images from the day. He kept seeing images of the cross, but instead of Yeshua he was looking at himself nailed to it. But in his dream, he was also an observer. At one point he woke up suddenly, not knowing where he was. It was still dark, and he could feel the lengths of wood underneath him painfully sticking into his body. Was he actually on the cross? He leapt up falling off the logs onto the ground in a panic. He spent the rest of the night propped up against the wall of the woodshed, going over the events of the previous day. The reality was even worse than his nightmare.

Where was Judas? What had happened to him? Simon sat there with tears rolling down his face, feeling utterly wretched.

When first light began to break, he felt sufficiently hungry and thirsty to brave an approach to the hostel to see if he could get something to eat and drink. It was still dark and very quiet. The hostel was locked, so he sat on a bench outside biding his time.

In the quiet he became aware of the sound of trickling water. It didn't take him long to locate a small stream and, in a pool, he was able to fill his water bottle before drinking it down and refilling it. He returned to the bench still hungry, but at least he was no longer thirsty. As he took his seat the door opened and a middle-aged lady came out.

'What are you doing here?' she asked, looking startled.

'I was passing through and wondered if you might have anything to eat? If it's not too much trouble? I would be happy to pay,' he asked feebly.

'It's *Pesach* you know! We don't serve food on a Sabbath!' she scolded patronisingly, suspecting him to be some sort of religious type, but then she thought a minute.

'I do have some *Matzot* left over from the *Seder*, I made some extra in case we had a last-minute traveller, but no one showed up. Would you like some?'

Simon jumped at the suggestion.

'That would be very acceptable. Thank you kindly,' he got up and came towards the door, but she disappeared inside shutting the door behind her. She wasn't about to admit him as a resident on the Sabbath. He was impressed.

A minute later she returned and, opening the door, placed a large plate of unleavened bread on the ground outside and closed the door without saying a word. Simon ate most of it and stuffed the rest into his travelling bag, leaving the empty plate by the door. He left a little money next to it to cover her costs, but in such a way that it looked like a gift.

The next question was what to do with his time without transgressing the Sabbath?

He decided to go and sit by the stream. There was nothing else to do.

The stream was busy emptying itself of the recent rain, and as it did so Simon turned over in his mind the extraordinary events of the past couple of years. It had been a time in his life like no other and he had been privileged to be an eyewitness to a large part of it.

He thought about Yeshua dying in such a gruesome way, his blood overlaid on the blood of countless criminals, running down the upright post of the cross. It reminded him of the lamb's blood at the first Passover being painted onto the door posts of the Israelites to ward off the angel of death.

He thought about the Israelite's flight out of Egypt and his flight out of Jerusalem. Would G_d deliver him like he delivered Israel from the pursuing Egyptians? He hoped he would.

He thought about Judas, his only son, and how he hated himself for what he had done to him. He longed for truth to be restored but he had a bad feeling about Judas and what might have befallen him. He feared he might be too late, but he was not about to make any enquiries.

Yeshua was gone. So, what would happen now?

He felt depressed and alone, staring into the little pool in front of him. His vision blurred with tears of regret and disappointment. His life was a similar blur, and he wasn't sure where it would lead now. Everything had seemed so settled before any of this had happened. But for the moment he had only one thing to worry about and that was survival.

Despite the Sabbath, he would head for the town of Lydda, where he hoped to find a teaching job. Lydda was well known as a seat of learning, although he had never been there himself. A while back he had heard that the synagogue had been looking for a teacher at the school, since their resident teacher had been crippled by a stroke and unable to carry out his duties.

It was difficult to fill such vacancies outside Jerusalem. It was unlikely there would be much pay as such, but perhaps it might prove a useful stop gap for Simon. He would at least get his board and lodging covered and it would be something to do. He did have a little money saved up for a rainy day and this, after all, was a very rainy day.

1 **Note:** Until 1968, when an archaeological discovery made by Vassilios Tzaferis who was investigating some tombs discovered during building work in Jerusalem, no physical evidence had ever been found to substantiate exactly how victims of Roman crucifixion were secured to the cross. In the case of this victim the osteological evidence suggested that his feet were nailed through both ankles, the nail entering from the right side of the ankle. The nail was held in place by a wooden washer to stop the head pulling out. He was secured to the patibulum crossbeam by further nails through each forearm just above the wrist. Some additional means of support must have been provided by a small seat or sedile which he probably sat on while his legs were twisted sideways with his knees drawn up and to the left. The single nail passing through his ankles had apparently hit a knot in the olive wood upright stake of the cross and buckled over making it impossible to remove from his feet when he was taken down from the cross after his death. A piece of olive wood was still trapped in the buckled tip of the nail. The date was assessed to be the Second Temple period which was also the period in which the crucifixion of Christ took place. Also visible on the remains was clear evidence that the shin bones had been shattered against the stake of the cross presumably to bring his ordeal to a close, a practice referred to in the gospel accounts.

Chapter 18

# A CHANCE TO START AGAIN

With the Sabbath behind them, the people of Jerusalem were returning to their normal activities, and Caiaphas was busy holding a meeting of the Lower Sanhedrin. Yeshua the Nazarene had
been successfully prosecuted and executed, but now there were
disturbing rumours that he had been seen alive in the city.

This was Caiaphas' worst nightmare.

He had gone out of his way to pre-empt this event by posting
guards on the tomb, and the Council was now being told by the
Captain of the Guard that not only had Simon Ish Kerioth escaped
his extensive attempts at capture, but a crucified, dead and buried man, placed in a tomb with a huge stone over the entrance,
had disappeared! The week was not getting off to a great start.

Caiaphas was furious. 'Are you telling me that my own Guard,
the Guard of the Temple of Israel, when given the simple task of
guarding a dead body, let it get up and walk out! You blithering
idiots! What do you take me for? How difficult is it for you to
guard a dead body for heaven's sake?

'I can just about grasp how a group of total imbeciles could
let an old man like Simon Ish Kerioth give them the slip, but to
let a dead man walk out of his tomb right under your stupid nos-
es? Are you seriously asking me to believe a cock and bull story about an angel and an earthquake? If we are to believe that,
we'll believe anything!'

The Council grilled the captain in detail, but he stood his
ground and stuck to his account. Eventually they agreed that the
body must have been stolen by his disciples, but even that didn't
make any sense. Joseph of Arimathea, who had made available
his own personal tomb for the resting place of Yeshua, came under a lot of suspicion but said nothing. He had been staying with

Annas, a former high priest and father-in-law of Caiaphas, since before Passover, a rock-solid alibi.

The meeting broke up with Caiaphas storming out in a rage, uttering black threats against the guards and against Simon Ish Kerioth.

By contrast, Joseph was seen leaving with the faintest wisp of a smile on his face and a visible spring in his step.

Meanwhile Simon headed west, living rough for a day or so and keeping his head down. On the way to Joppa, he stopped at an inn, where he saw a notice for temporary work in the local citrus harvest. He would be able to lie low for a while before making his way to Lydda. He had helped his father in Kerioth as a lad and always enjoyed being outside in the groves.

The job led to some further work there and he stayed in the area for just over six months before departing with his cash reserves replenished, albeit by not very much.

A day or so later a dishevelled looking grey-haired man walked into the synagogue in Lydda and asked for the rabbi. He introduced himself simply as Simon. He asked if any teaching jobs were available in the town. He had taken the precaution of looking down the notice board in the entrance to make sure there was no one attached to the synagogue whom he might know. He told the rabbi he was from Capernaum.

The rabbi, a kind-looking old man, seemed pleased to hear that Simon was looking for work in the school and, noticing his newly acquired rough hands, didn't ask him too many questions. He seemed much more concerned about a recent development that had upset his traditional way of life.

Some of his people had taken to adopting a rising interest in the teachings of the man from Nazareth who had been crucified earlier in the year and who, some claimed, had risen from the dead. They purported to have met some of his disciples, who claimed to have seen him alive after his death. Whether he was a prophet or not, he couldn't tell, but apparently he had demonstrated miraculous signs and wonders during his lifetime – or so they said.

'Did you ever come across him in Capernaum?' he enquired.

'I did indeed hear about him, and I witnessed the great crowds that followed him,' responded Simon trying not to give too much away. 'It was the talk of the town, Rabbi,' he added.

'Well, yes, indeed. Talk's a fine thing, but Messiah? Doesn't sound like the Messiah to me, I'm afraid,' the rabbi dismissed the subject. 'Now, I take it you can start pretty much straight away?' the rabbi continued. Simon nodded. 'I think if you were to visit Aeneas, who looks after the school and used to teach there before his illness, he may be able to give you some board and lodging. He lives just beyond the school, down this road on the right-hand side,' and he fetched a small offcut of a scroll from a drawer in his desk and wrote a quick reference for Simon to take to Aeneas.

'Here, take this note to him by way of introduction.' The rabbi handed him the note and Simon thanked him profusely before departing in search of Aeneas.

There had been quite an explosion of those turning to the Messianic faith in Yeshua shortly after his death. A purge by the authorities had resulted in a man named Stephen, a prominent leader, being stoned to death following false accusations against him. Consequently, many of the new converts had dispersed to the regions, taking their new message with them. Instead of dampening down enthusiasm, the dispersal had resulted in quite the opposite effect.

So many miraculous healings and signs of great power had been occurring all over the country at the hands of these disciples that most synagogues had at least some people who had accepted Yeshua as their long-awaited Messiah. New believers saw in his death a sacrifice of redemption for those who could accept it. They also believed the reports that Yeshua's tomb had been found empty and that he had been seen alive as if he had risen from the dead.

Nevertheless, Simon found himself in a difficult predicament. On the one hand, he was wanted by the Jewish authorities on a series of trumped-up charges and for what they saw as theft of evidence they had paid for and thus Temple property. The fact that the scrolls might provide incriminating evidence of the High

Priest's methods was incidental. On the other hand, he was far from certain that he would be accepted by these new Messianic followers, whose Messiah he had conspired to have arrested. He therefore resolved to maintain a degree of anonymity, but at the same time he was desperate to make sure that his evidence found its way into the right hands where it could be appreciated.

Walking down the street in search of Aeneas he turned these two juxtapositions over in his mind. Reconciling them was not going to be straightforward.

He found Aeneas' house as described and was ushered in by a helper. Aeneas lay on a low bed on the ground floor. Not only was his right side virtually paralysed, making it impossible to stand for any length of time, but his speech had been impeded by his illness and he was difficult to understand. But he seemed a nice man and was very pleased to see Simon. He offered Simon lodgings as part of the job and soon they were enjoying a new friendship with many common interests.

Aeneas' speech impediment was to prove a useful way of deflecting unwanted questions. Simon would just pretend not to understand and change the subject. He quickly became adept at doing this, but the two men seemed to get on well together and as Simon's teaching proved invaluable in the school, no one cared too much about his elusive past.

But Simon knew that he was a wanted man and so he was happy to remain anonymous.

Life was settling down well for Simon until one evening when Aeneas' had invited some of his Messianic friends for a meal. Marcus, one of the friends, mentioned that he had just heard that they were shortly to receive a visit by one of the most senior disciples of Yeshua. Peter was coming to Lydda on a tour of the region. This was disastrous news for Simon, as he realised he would immediately be recognised. They asked him if he had ever met Peter since they had both been in Capernaum. Simon suddenly found himself in a bit of a fix. There was only one solution, and he casually expressed his disappointment that he wouldn't be there as he had decided to visit a friend in the next town.

'I dithn't know yu had frienths nearby. Woo they be thome-one I migh know?' he enquired in his laborious drawl.

'Oh, I doubt it, my friend,' replied Simon smartly navigating round the question. 'My real friends are you and the brothers here!' he jested. 'No, this is just an old friend I knew years ago. He may not live there anymore, but I thought I would go and see. I will be back before the term begins,' and before anyone could say any more, he quickly asked a question.

'When is Peter due to arrive?' he enquired.

'He wiwll be heer in thime for the Thabbath,' stumbled Aeneas, hoping he could persuade his friend to stay and hear him. He felt sure it would help him in his quest for the truth. 'Ih woo be a thame to mith him. Hith a vewry good thpeaker, yoo know.'

'Well, you never know, my friend may not be there, and I might get back in time to see Peter. I will be gone early tomorrow so must get some rest. Goodnight, Aeneas. Goodnight everyone.' He rose to his feet and left the room for bed without any further discussion. Nobody knew what to make of it all and they just sat there looking at one another.

'Ee thtruglth wiv thith thort of thin.' Aeneas took so long to get the sentence out that the others couldn't contain themselves and burst out laughing at the irony of his comment. Fortunately, Aeneas had a good sense of humour and saw the funny side, joining in, snorting and hooting with laughter.

Life was very difficult for Aeneas. Apart from home help, he needed assistance every time he wanted to go out, for example to the synagogue. The other Jews had taken a rather hard line and felt that his paralysis was due to sin. The rabbi, interestingly, did not make his views known, but was always on hand to help Aeneas as a friend and not just his rabbi. Aeneas was very grateful to the rabbi.

The Messianic Jews, on the other hand, held a totally different view according to the revolutionary teaching of Yeshua. They saw Aeneas as a brother and someone who G_d cared about deeply, and they prayed for his healing regularly. To date, nothing had changed, but that didn't seem to matter to them. They carried on tending to him and praying for him in the eternal hope that he would be healed, if not in this world, then in the next. Their blind faith drew quite a bit of derision from some of the other members of the congregation, but they didn't seem to mind.

As one senior member of the synagogue put it, 'If G_d wanted to heal him he would just do it. The fact that he doesn't is a clear indication that his sin remains.'

There were endless debates between the two factions in the synagogue, particularly about Aeneas and whether he should be allowed to come into the men's area in the synagogue in his sinful state. Apart from agreeing that he would get in the way, the rabbi took no side in this debate, but it was agreed that he could lie on his bed inside the entrance as a compromise. Like all compromises, it satisfied no one, and so the debate continued.

Simon never returned in time to hear Peter. He was determined to avoid being recognised.

So when Peter did come to visit, Aeneas was brought to the Synagogue and placed in his usual place just inside the entrance where he could hear but could not see.

Peter began his address in front of a packed synagogue of Jews, not only from Lydda but the whole surrounding area. He spoke for a good hour, but the people hung on every word.

He began by speaking about the prophets of old who had foretold the coming of the Messiah. He showed how they had spoken of a suffering servant and how Yeshua had fulfilled those prophecies in his death on the cross as well as the fulfilment of many other prophecies. He went on to talk about Yeshua being like a corner stone of a new building that was being put together with living stones and how he had become a rock of offence that many Jews were stumbling over as they struggled to accept this interpretation of scripture.

He then affirmed to all Jews that they were a chosen race, a Royal Priesthood, indeed a Holy Nation, a people for G_d's own possession, called out of darkness into the most marvellous light and that they had received mercy.

He spoke about the life and teaching of Yeshua and how he had suffered death by crucifixion in order to bring restoration and forgiveness to his people. He went on to say that after being buried in a nearby tomb that he, Peter, had run to the grave and found it empty, but following appearances to his disciples they realised he had risen from the dead. Then he sent his Holy Spirit on the disciples at Pentecost, giving them strength and confidence to take the good news out to the world.

Peter spoke with such conviction and of course from personal experience that he captivated his listeners. He had a radiance about him which seemed to fill the whole synagogue. But when he invited members to accept Yeshua as Messiah the mood changed; some responded, but many others refused.

Then something happened which would change everything.

On his way out, Peter caught sight of Aeneas lying on the floor just inside the entrance. He stopped and just stood there looking at Aeneas. As he did so, Aeneas began to feel a sort of warmth inside and a sense of peace coming over him in a totally unfamiliar way. The intensity of this experience increased to the point where he felt his entire body aglow, and he wasn't sure if he was there in the synagogue or if he was somewhere else entirely. It was so strange that by rights he should have been frightened, but he wasn't.

Meanwhile, Peter did no more than look at him. It felt like a long time to Aeneas, but to those watching it didn't seem that long at all. Those who were jostling to leave the synagogue just stopped and stared, everyone fell silent and in the silence Peter's disciples could be heard praying softly, some of them in languages other than their own. It was if they knew what was going to happen next.

Then Peter crouched down next to Aeneas and asked him his name, enquiring about his condition. He then rose to his feet and spoke firmly to him.

'Aeneas, Yeshua Messiah heals you. Gather up your bed things and get up.'

Aeneas felt as if he was dreaming. The presence of G_d was so overwhelming, he barely noticed Peter, who was holding out his hand to him. Without even thinking about it, he made to get up. First he raised himself up on his elbows and rolled over onto his side before turning over into the kneeling position. Then he struggled to his feet, using muscles he hadn't used for eight long years. Eventually, he stood unsteadily but upright in front of Peter, and the two men just stood there looking at each other.

It suddenly dawned on him that he was actually standing upright on his own without any assistance! He looked down at his trembling legs and feet and held out his cupped hands in front of him with incredulity. He could move his right arm normally. Slowly he turned his hands over and you could hear people gasp.

Aeneas began to laugh. At first not much more than a whisper, but then with each breath the volume increased until he was literally roaring with uncontrollable laughter!

The people around him began to laugh too, not that they found it funny or embarrassing. It was more like pure joy! The more Aeneas laughed the more everyone else laughed, until the whole synagogue was in uproar with laughter! It was like a river pouring out from Aeneas. Peter was laughing and so were all his disciples. Even the Rabbi was laughing.

Then Aeneas' laughing began to subside, his bottom lip started to quiver, and his face screwed up. His chest heaved with great sobs and tears rolled down his face. He could feel his heart fit to burst with emotions of thankfulness and pure joy bubbling up from somewhere, he didn't know where.

He sank to his knees, reaching out to Peter.

People next to him, thinking he had collapsed, reached out to him, but he had hold of Peter's cloak and was thanking him over and over again. But Peter backed away, telling him to direct his thanks to the risen Yeshua, who had been his true healer, and not to him. Those closest to Aeneas realized he was speaking normally, but Peter didn't even know he had an impediment. Everyone was truly amazed.

That day was an unforgettable day. There was such a buzz all over town. They had heard about Yeshua healing people but never thought that would happen in their own town. People could talk about nothing else for days. The picture of Aeneas walking falteringly back to his house, carrying his own bedding, surrounded by a crowd of people wanting to see him and talk to him, would stay in people's minds for the rest of their lives.

The celebrations went on for over a week and so many people turned up to the synagogue the following Saturday that they couldn't fit everyone in!

Simon had heard that Peter had moved on and decided it was safe to return. He walked into the house and was met by enthusiastic reports of what had taken place. Aeneas was sitting upright on a bench by the window. He got up and came towards Simon to greet him. Simon could barely believe his eyes!

'Welcome back, my friend!' Aeneas spoke in a perfectly normal voice unfamiliar to Simon. He had not known him before his illness, so it was like meeting him for the first time. His speech had fully returned to normal.

'We have much to share with you. This has been an incredible time!' Simon sat down, speechless, and they told him the whole story. He simply didn't know what to say.

Later that evening when everyone had left, he made Aeneas something to eat as he had done many times before and they sat and chatted late into the night. Aeneas shared in detail everything that had happened.

'You know, Simon. Last Sabbath when I went to the synagogue it wasn't just my illness that was healed, it was all of me. I felt totally free. Everyone I met seemed so alive! I was aware of every part of G_d's creation. The trees, the birds, everything. There is so much to be thankful for. I can't stop praising G_d!' Aeneas poured out his thoughts to Simon. 'I can't remember when I last walked into the Synagogue and took my place with everyone else. I got so used to being carried to the entrance porch where I had to strain to hear what was being said inside. But now I'm no longer a sick 'sinner'! I am free now!

'I am so grateful, Simon!' he repeated it over and over again.

Simon sat and listened, soaking up every word. The change in Aeneas was truly remarkable.

But then his thoughts turned to the little leather case upstairs hidden away. Inside were the scrolls. Simon had sat in front of Yeshua and recorded the very words he was speaking, straight from his mouth. And here was Aeneas talking about Yeshua as if he had met him personally! It was bizarre. It was if he had actually met with Yeshua; not dead but alive!

Simon was now bursting to share his own story with his friend Aeneas, but something still held him back. Was it the warrant out for his arrest? Was it the rumours of agents from Jerusalem still charged with finding him? Was it the many new believers in Yeshua Messiah, like Aeneas, who spoke out and were being arrested and dragged back to Jerusalem for trial? He didn't know. The jails in Jerusalem were full to the brim and some had been stoned to death by quango courts and rabble crowds.

One Pharisee who had gone about his work with particular determination had been present at one of these stonings. He was a young man named Saul from Tarsus. He was very aggressive in his pursuit of this new faith, which he saw as the Great Blasphemy. Simon imagined that his own name would be on one of Saul's lists.

What made him particularly afraid of Saul was that he knew him from his studies under Gamaliel. Saul was much younger, but he remembered him as extremely ambitious and determined. He did not relish being confronted by Saul, who would probably recognise him.

Retiring to bed that night, Simon went to the cupboard where he had hidden the leather case. He took it down and withdrew the scrolls. Spreading them out on a small table by the window. With his lamp on the windowsill, he began to read the first one. He hadn't even opened the case since he left Jerusalem on the day of the crucifixion.

The one on the top was headed, 'Capernaum – Leaders Gathering at Peter's home.'

Simon recalled the day well. It had started with Yeshua answering questions from the audience but then the subject changed to forgiveness, and he had been talking about G_d's forgiving nature.

It had all been reasonably good natured up to that point, but the mood was changing. He recalled that some men had clambered onto the roof, dug a big hole in the fabric and lowered down a paralysed man right in front of Yeshua.

He crouched down and told him his sins were forgiven. Well, that did it. Everyone was objecting. People were accusing him of outright blasphemy.

Simon looked at the scroll. He read out the words he had written down, which were the very words spoken by Yeshua, and the curious thing was that they seemed to come alive to him. It was as if Yeshua was there in the room with him.

'Friend, your sins are forgiven.' Simon read it several times. It was as if Yeshua was speaking, not just to that paralysed man, and to all who were paralysed, including Aeneas, but even directly to Simon! He read on and saw that he had recorded the words that many people were muttering, particularly a man next to him. He had said indignantly, 'Only G_d can forgive sins!'

As he read on, Yeshua's words spoke again. 'Why are you reasoning in your hearts? Which is easier to say? "Your sins are forgiven" or to say, "Rise and walk"? But in order that you may know that the Son of Man has authority on earth to forgive sins,' and he turned to the paralysed man and said, 'Get up, pick up your mattress and go home.'

Simon thought about Peter and what Aeneas had recounted about Peter's words to him; 'Yeshua heals you.'

Then he thought about all the things he had done wrong in his life and how far away he felt from G_d compared to Aeneas and his friends. Their joy said it all.

He felt incredibly sorry for what he had done. He read again the words Yeshua had uttered that day in Capernaum. 'Friend, your sins are forgiven.' A tear rolled down his nose and dropped onto the scroll, smudging the ink slightly. Simon instinctively reached for the small piece of cloth he kept in the carry case and mopped his tear off the word 'sins' where it had landed.

Some of the ink was absorbed into the cloth. The word 'sins' was still legible on the scroll and a part of it was now also on his cloth as a dark smudge, but the word was no longer recognisable on the cloth. He poured a little water into his washing bowl and rinsed the cloth in the clean water, squeezing it out and observing that it was now completely clean. He pondered the significance of this.

He recalled the scripture he knew so well from the first chapter of Isaiah. 'Come let us settle the matter, though your sins are like scarlet they shall be as white as snow.'

Simon held up the clean cloth against the little flame from his lamp. The light shone right through it with no sign of any ink. It was as white as wool.

Pictures of Yeshua filled his mind. He saw him on the cross, his head hung forward, his last breath exhaling. All the suffering and pain gone. It was he, Simon, who should have died there, but he didn't. It was if Yeshua carried all Simon's pain and sin away by an act of perfect sacrifice. Better than a thousand burnt offerings. The Father's own son, like Isaac on the altar with his father Abraham ready to sacrifice him, but no, G_d says 'Let it be *my* son!'

He was about to roll up the scrolls to put them away when he saw one other thing he had written. It was a comment made by the man next to him that day in Capernaum.

It read simply, 'We have seen remarkable things today.' He remembered how those words had struck him when he heard them.

He rolled up the scrolls and returned the case to its hiding place before retiring to bed. He blew out the lamp and lay back with his hand behind his head.

'Remarkable things indeed,' he whispered to himself. Within minutes he was fast asleep.

The next day he rose early. He had made up his mind. He would confide everything in his friend Aeneas. He would tell him the whole story and then he would show him the scrolls.

Chapter 19

# COMING CLEAN

It was late summer in Joppa. A cool breeze blew in off the Mediterranean Sea and across the sand dunes.

Peter and John Mark, together with a group of Peter's disciples, were staying with a man called Simon, who had a leather business at the back of his house. They were waiting for lunch and Peter had gone up onto the roof of the house to find a quiet place to pray.

It was around midday and the heat inside the house was getting unbearably hot. He found the smell of cooking combined with the smell of the tannery not much to his liking. He was used to the smell of fish, but there was something about the smell of leather which he didn't care for.

He liked being on the roof. It reminded him of home, in a way. There was a rather tattered old awning held together by strips of leather and an old wicker reclining chair which was incredibly comfortable.

He made himself at home in the old wicker chair looking out to sea.

The breeze clipped the crest of the waves, the sun dancing along the white spume. It reminded Peter of Galilee, out on a boat on the sea, the wind tilting the hull, drawing it gently through the water.

He tried to focus his mind to pray for the mission he was involved with, but the low murmur of the waves breaking against the shore and the sound of seagulls crying out to one another distracted him away from his purpose. His thoughts turned to the time spent with Yeshua, moving from one community to another. It was a time like no other and full of fun and excitement. Then there was the traumatic time in Jerusalem when Yeshua seemed to play into the hands of his captors, which resulted in his death. But of all the miracles which he had witnessed, the miracle of the resurrection would stay with him forever.

For Peter, he would probably still be fishing if Yeshua hadn't intervened. It was a time of deep healing for him and enabled him to be in the right place when the Holy Spirit fell on him and the other disciples at Pentecost. That single event was what changed them all from an apprehensive group of well-meaning and obedient followers into a dynamic, emboldened, and enabled force for the Kingdom of G_d. It quite literally sparked off a revolution.

He leant back in the old wicker chair, the warm breeze ruffling his beard and the enticing smell of lunch wafting up from below, making him feel hungry.

Before he knew it, he was drifting off into a blissful sleep.

And then the dreams began. At first, he couldn't make much sense of them, but then he had a very striking dream.

There was a huge sheet being lowered down in front of him and when it got low enough to see inside, it made him jump. It was full of every conceivable creepy crawly and unclean creature imaginable. As he recoiled, he heard a voice urging him to kill and eat them. The thought revolted him, but the voice urged him on and warned him not to call the things that G_d had cleansed, unclean. He woke up with a start, but he could still see the unfolding dream; it persisted until the sheet was lifted back up out of sight.

Sweat was trickling down his brow.

'What on earth was that all about?' he muttered to himself and while he was going over the dream in his mind, he heard loud voices below.

He got up and peered over the parapet. He could see two men and a soldier at the gate. They were calling for Simon the Tanner. At first he was apprehensive, but then he saw the maid going out and talking to them. They seemed quite friendly. He was about to resume his time of prayer when he felt a strong sense that the Holy Spirit was directing him to go wherever the men wanted him to go.

He went down to meet the visitors.

'I think I'm the person you're looking for,' said Peter, walking up to the men who were still outside the gate, 'how can I help?'

The men explained that their boss, a centurion in the Roman army living in Caesarea, had experienced a vision directing him to send for a man named Peter at this address.

'Yes, that's me,' said Peter. Then, without consulting anyone, he calmly invited the three Gentile men in to eat with them and stay the night as guests in Simon the Tanner's house. At first a few eyebrows were raised, but everyone respected Peter's judgement and so nothing was said.

The next day they all set off early for Caesarea.

Cornelius had everything ready for their arrival. His relatives and close friends were all there to greet Peter, so the house was full. He greeted Peter as if he was a god, but Peter quickly put him right and asked to be treated like any other. It was the first time Peter had ever stepped inside a Gentile house and he most certainly didn't feel like a god.

The reception room was quite spacious, but not big enough for everyone, so some people had to stand in the atrium at the centre of the house.

Peter took up a position near the door where everyone could hear. Cornelius introduced Peter and explained why he had invited him to deliver the message which he was sure G_d had given him and then he handed the meeting over to Peter.

In truth Peter didn't really have a message as such, but relying on the Holy Spirit of Yeshua to guide him, he started by explaining his dream and how he had interpreted it to mean that G_d wanted to start a change in the way Jews and Gentiles related to one another. He felt the circumstances surrounding his presence with them that day were clear guidance that G_d wanted to break down those barriers and deal with all men as equals.

Peter went on to relate the reasons why they were followers of Yeshua Messiah and how those who believe in him receive forgiveness of their sins.

As he was still speaking, it became apparent that the Holy Spirit was moving among the people who were there, and very soon the Spirit was falling on everyone. They were even speaking in tongues and praising G_d, just like the day of Pentecost. The Jews who had come with Peter stood there in amazement. They couldn't quite take in what they were seeing. It was astonishing. They had often witnessed such scenes among Jewish believers, but never among non-Jews.

Peter seemed less perturbed and ordered water to be brought for baptism. It was quite a party, and after all the celebrations Peter and his disciples were invited to stay on for a few days.

# Chapter 20

## NO TURNING BACK

When Simon Ish Kerioth woke up, the sun had risen, and he realised he had overslept. He could hear Aeneas downstairs and smell
the aroma of freshly baked bread. He washed and descended to
join his friend and over one shoulder he carried the scroll case.

'I've got something to share with you, Aeneas,' he began.

Aeneas turned around briefly from what he was doing to acknowledge Simon.

'Oh?' he asked, 'I think I know what that might be. But do
please go on.'

Simon looked at him closely. Surely he hadn't been snooping
in his room, had he? There was an awkward silence for a moment. Aeneas was still standing with his back to Simon preparing some food.

'You've been on the run from the Holy Spirit. You know, he
will get to you in the end!' he chided, turning around to face
Simon.

'It's true, isn't it, Simon?' he asked.

'Well, that's part of it I agree, but you don't know the other part.' He sat down at the table and began to unpack his carry
case. He rolled out the scrolls onto the table, securing the ends
open with a couple of bowls of fruit.

Aeneas interrupted. 'Before you explain, there is something
I need to tell you. We had word from Peter that something truly amazing has happened with the Romans in Caesarea. So,
Marcus and a couple of the others plan to set off there in about
half an hour. Why don't you come with us, and you can tell us
the whole story as we travel?'

Simon was a little put out. He had steeled himself for this moment and now Aeneas didn't seem that interested!

'What have you got there?' Aeneas asked, looking down at the scrolls.

'It's a long story, my friend, and it will take me quite a long time to explain.' He rolled up the scrolls and returned them to the case. Aeneas laid out some food and after Simon had given a blessing they sat down to eat.

'I would love to come with you,' Simon broke the silence after a moment or two. 'It won't take me long to gather up my things and I will explain everything on the way. But tell me this Aeneas. Are you fit enough to travel to Caesarea? It's quite a long way.'

'Oh, I think so, really I do. I have been practising walking daily and I can feel the strength returning daily,' he said with a smile. 'I am sure that the Lord can take care of me, just as he healed me. I feel amazingly well.'

Simon thought for a moment. 'Alright,' he said, 'but before we go, don't you want to know what I've got in this case?' He was dying to tell Aeneas and was not going to let it be delayed a second longer.

'Well, I can see you are going to tell me anyway!' he laughed.

'What you were looking at a few moments ago is…' and he paused before committing himself further, because what he was about to say didn't trip off his lips readily. 'What you saw was the word of G_d, the bread of life.' He picked up a piece of bread and broke it in two before giving Aeneas one half.

'These words were taken down personally by me while I was following Yeshua in Galilee, and they are all his words. The words of eternal life.

'But there is a twist, and that is going to take me quite a while to explain.'

Aeneas looked at him with disbelief.

'Are you saying you were following Yeshua Messiah before he was crucified? That's truly extraordinary! How come you haven't mentioned this before?'

Simon turned his piece of bread over and over in his hands studying it carefully.

'Yes, I did follow him,' he whispered almost inaudibly, and then he looked up at his friend. 'Shall we prepare to depart, my brother, and I'll explain all on the way? You're right, it is extraordinary.' Simon hadn't referred to Aeneas as his 'brother' before, and just using the word made a profound impression on him.

Aeneas stood up. 'I can't wait. It'll keep me moving as we go. I'm due to meet the others outside the synagogue in a short while.'

The two men gathered up what they needed for the journey and headed up to the synagogue.

They decided to break their journey with one stop using the coast road. It would make it easier for Aeneas. The overall journey would be around thirty miles. If Aeneas felt up to it, they could go further on the first day and arrive sooner. They didn't want to miss Peter and were unsure how long he would be staying in Caesarea.

On the road, their three traveling companions, Marcus, Junias, and Silvanus, walked quite a distance ahead, with Aeneas and Simon bringing up the rear. The three were talking animatedly among themselves, unaware that Simon had started to unfold his full story to Aeneas.

Aeneas had no idea about Simon's past and was amazed to hear the full story. Actually, he was quite shocked that he had been living so long with someone whom he had trusted but who had been involved in the betrayal of Yeshua Messiah. He had no idea that Simon was a scribe. He had suspected he was well-educated, on account of the excellent teaching skills he had demonstrated to the pupils at the school. He had been a popular teacher with the students, and no one had thought to ask.

Simon confessed to everything. He kept nothing back and by the time he had finished he felt as if a great weight had been lifted off his shoulders.

'So now you know everything, Aeneas, and I feel I owe you an apology for not being open with you from the start, but I hope you understand why I couldn't do that, and I beg you to forgive me.'

The two men continued walking in silence. Simon was afraid he had damaged a beautiful friendship by being so devious.

Aeneas called out to the three men ahead. There was a small stone bridge ahead over a dried-up stream.

'I think we will take a short break at that bridge ahead,' he called out. The three men were nearly there and so they sat down to rest and waited for Aeneas and Simon to catch up.

'How are your legs, Aeneas?' asked Marcus.

'Oh, they're fine thank you,' replied Aeneas dropping down onto the parapet of the little bridge.

'But I could do with a drink. I'm very thirsty.' They all sparingly took a drink from the leather water bottles they had brought with them.

Simon was very conscious that Aeneas had not said anything yet about his confession. Now they were all together, it was a bit awkward to ask him.

'Friends,' asked Aeneas, 'What's the worst thing you have ever done in your life?'

There was an awkward silence.

'Why do you want to know?' asked Silvanus.

'Well, has anyone done something which was so bad that Yeshua would not forgive it?' Aeneas looked around at his friends and finally back to Simon. They all looked a bit puzzled. 'OK, so how many times do you think we ought to forgive each other, or are there sins against each other that we cannot forgive?' No one seemed any the wiser but Simon was beginning to get the point.

Aeneas turned and looked straight at Simon.

'You see Simon, Yeshua died for our sin, period. He has forgiven us for everything. Therefore, we must forgive every brother everything as many times as we have to. Would we all agree?'

The other three looked at one another and just shrugged their shoulders in agreement.

'Yes, of course we agree,' said Marcus.

Aeneas smiled at Simon, 'Simon, I would probably have done the same thing as you did in your circumstances, but even if not, it makes no difference, I fully forgive you.

'So, I think it's time we went on, don't you?' He rose to his feet, embracing Simon warmly, and they set off once again.

This time Aeneas and Simon led the way while the other three held back a little.

'What was that all about?' asked Junias.

'I have no idea,' replied Silvanus, looking at Marcus for inspiration.

'Neither have I.' Marcus shrugged, and the three of them walked on in silence.

Two things still bothered Simon. No one seemed to know what had happened to Judas. Aeneas didn't know, and that meant that no news had reached this part of Israel.

The second thing that bothered him was not knowing how Peter would react to seeing him again. Would he turn Simon in? Perhaps he would, but somehow it didn't matter anymore. He had made a decision, and what was important now was being a part of this new body of believers. It was exciting and hugely comforting, and he was enjoying every minute.

The following day they set off from their overnight stop for the naval port of Caesarea. One thing they still needed to work out was just how to find the centurion's house.

Caesarea Maritima was a sprawling city with an artificial port built by Herod around forty-five years earlier. It was well laid out and ultra-modern. The officers' quarters were built to the highest standards, boasting all the latest thinking in architecture and house design. Fresh water was brought in by aqueduct from the foot of Mount Carmel, some six or seven miles away.

The Roman quarter was extensive, being the civil and military administrative headquarters for the Judean Provence and the seat and official residence of the Roman Prefect, Pontius Pilate.

Five Jewish men made their way nervously towards the outskirts of this overtly Roman city, aware that they were followers of one who had been put to death at the hands of this selfsame authority. They prayed for both protection and guidance.

The Jewish sector was reassuringly familiar. Along the road outside the city, they found themselves in a small makeshift marketplace with stall holders on either side of the road.

Approaching one of the stallholders Simon tentatively asked for directions to the military quarter.

'Who are you looking for?' he enquired.

'We're looking for a Roman centurion by the name of Cornelius, but I don't suppose you will know who he is,' said Simon nervously.

'Cornelius?' he asked, 'Do you mean the Cornelius who invited Peter the Galilean to his house the other day?'

'Yes, that's right,' responded Simon, looking surprised. 'That would be him.'

The man leant forward, looking right and left as if to be careful not to be overheard. He then took a step back and in a loud voice for all to hear he bellowed, 'You, my friends, must be the only people around here who don't know where he lives!'

He was joined by his neighbouring stallholders in raucous laughter. Clearly, Aeneas and his friends were not the first people to visit Caesarea asking for Cornelius, and this had quickly become a standing joke.

The laughter subsided, and the man jovially came round the front of his stall to give them detailed directions.

Eventually they were on their way, fully briefed with instructions as to the exact location of the now famous house, and a short while later they arrived outside a well-kept, smart looking residence answering the description given them.

None of them had ever been inside a non-Jewish home before, let alone a Roman one. The avenue was spaciously laid out with uniform single-storey villas under red pantile roofs, all painted white and set back a little from the road. The gardens were well-tended, dotted here and there with mature date palms. It was unlike anything any of them had seen before.

Attached to the house in a small porch, was a guard who was studiously watching them.

'Is this the residence of Cornelius the Centurion?' enquired Simon in his best Latin.

'And who might be asking?' came the reply.

Aeneas stepped forward. His Latin was a bit rusty, but he knew enough to get by.

'We were hoping to speak to Peter, the Galilean, if it's not too much trouble. My name is Aeneas from Lydda, and these are my travelling companions.'

The guard disappeared inside, returning a moment later followed by the larger-than-life frame of Peter, who brushed past the guard and warmly embraced Aeneas, greeting him like a long-lost friend. He squeezed him so tightly that Aeneas was afraid he would break a rib.

'May Yeshua be praised!' he exclaimed, looking Aeneas up and down, 'The last time we met, you were barely able to walk! But look at you now! Have you travelled all the way from Lydda unaided?' Aeneas, who was somewhat taken aback by this profuse welcome, nodded agreeably.

The five of them were ushered in and through to a small open courtyard where the other brothers were gathered. Cornelius was not at home but was due back shortly.

Aeneas introduced his companions one by one. Last was Simon. Aeneas was very conscious that this was not necessarily going to be an easy re-acquaintance. Peter had not taken note of him until now, but when their eyes met Peter stood there expressionless. There was an awkward silence as everyone sensed the situation had changed by the glare on Peter's face.

'I know you.' he said slowly. 'You are Simon the father of Judas Ish Kerioth.'

Nobody said a word or moved a muscle. All you could hear was the sound of the sea some distance beyond the villa and the rustle of the breeze in the top of a palm tree in the garden. Simon could feel all the apprehensions he thought he had left behind welling up inside him. It had evidently become common knowledge that he was Judas' father.

'I have been living with Aeneas in Lydda this past year or so,' he said feebly. He had rehearsed what he was going to say but it just didn't seem the right moment to explain. Peter's face was still expressionless. The tension had spread like a fire and all eyes were on Simon. Aeneas came to the rescue.

'Yes, Simon took my place in the school and helped to look after me before you visited Lydda and Yeshua healed me,' he explained. 'Simon was away when you came. But he has found the risen Yeshua for himself, I am sure of that, and has confessed all to me as we travelled here.' Peter looked back at Simon and studied his face. Simon felt a familiar sensation. He hadn't felt like this since he was face to face with Yeshua back in Capernaum. Peter mumbled something to himself. Was he praying or was he about to strike Simon? Simon was unclear, but it didn't matter to him.

'I will tell you everything, but I now know that Yeshua is the Messiah,' Simon confessed wringing his hands. His eyes were glazed with the raw emotion of a new-found love which was unfamiliar to him. He had always been the cool, collected man, firmly in control, scheming his way out of any situation, but now there was a fresh vulnerability to deal with, which he would need to get used to.

Peter's face changed. A beaming, great big smile spread across it like the sunrise. 'Well, that's alright then, isn't it?' he said calmly, looking around the gathered band of brothers who were not sure what was going to happen next. There was a brief lull while the new situation sunk in and then a rapturous applause broke out, with cheering and clapping that must have been audible halfway down the avenue. Peter stepped forward with his arms wide to welcome Simon. He gave him a huge bear hug. Simon was not that tall, and the embrace squeezed the breath out of him, but he was very thankful for the gesture from this man who was so much larger than life. Simon couldn't help noticing how he had changed. He was so much more self-assured than when he knew him before. There had been a huge change in him.

'Come, you must tell me the whole story,' Peter said, guiding Simon to a seat like a long-lost friend, 'but first there is something we have forgotten to do!' He summoned the maid and whispered something to her. She departed and soon returned with a towel over her arm and a bowl, in which stood a jug of fresh water. Peter took the bowl and the towel despite her protests. This was her job, she complained, but Peter reassured her that on this occasion it was going to be his. He knelt down in front of Simon, filled the bowl with water and removing Simon's sandals, proceeded to wash his feet. Simon was horrified and protested, but Peter looked up at him and calmly told him how Yeshua had done the same to him on the night before he died. Simon relaxed, and as he experienced this kindly act of love from the man who was now his leader, he reflected on his past. It brought to mind, too, how Anna had so kindly washed his feet whenever he returned from a long journey.

The experience was profoundly moving, and he found himself with tears tumbling down his face again, like unspoken prayers, washing away the past and refreshing his soul. When Peter had finished washing Aeneas and the other three friends, he introduced them all to the rest of Peter's disciples before taking Simon by the arm into one of the two rooms off the atrium.

He closed the door. Simon took out the carry case and removed the scrolls, sitting down at a small table in the middle of the room. Peter watched as he extracted the contents and spread them out on the table. Not a word was said as Peter studied the writing. 'Reading's not my strong point,' he confessed, 'Read it to me, what does it say?' Simon began to read a little, and as he did it was Peter's turn to weep. Listening to the very words that Yeshua had uttered, he could hear Yeshua's voice again. He stood up and went over to the shuttered window looking down the garden towards the sea. He listened, motionless, with tears rolling down his cheeks, recalling his time with his Lord and Master. When Simon stopped reading Peter turned to him.

'Did you write all that?' he asked pointing at the scrolls.

Simon told him the whole story from start to finish. Peter listened patiently, and when he had finished Simon rolled up the scrolls and returned them to the case, closing the lid and fastening the buckle. Telling the story had been a cathartic experience for both men and they sat there together, silently reminiscing.

'When I saw you writing on those wax notepads, I thought you were making notes for your own use. I had no idea that you were taking down Yeshua's exact words with a view to gathering evidence to give to Caiaphas to use against him.' Peter shook his head slowly. On one hand he could see the appalling treachery of what Simon had been doing, but on the other he could see the extraordinary grace of G_d in allowing that to happen because of his higher purpose. 'And all the while Yeshua must have known what you were actually doing! The Lord is so extraordinarily gracious. Can you see that, Simon?' Yes, he could see that, but although forgiveness buries the past everybody still remembers, so he just stared at the floor, he didn't know what to say. He felt ashamed of what he had done on one hand and yet profoundly forgiven on the other. He sat there thinking about it before breaking the silence.

'I would like to give these to you for safe keeping,' he said handing the case to Peter. 'The story needs to be told, and your help would be invaluable. It needs to be written down into a full account,' he suggested.

'That's really not my gifting,' said Peter turning the case over in his hands, 'but I would be happy to work with you and supply my own thoughts and recollections as required.' He handed the case back to Simon. 'That would be wonderful, I have thought long and hard about how to write it. Thank you.' He slung the case over his shoulder as the two men rose to re-join the others.

There was one last thing still troubling Simon, and Peter would surely have the answer. The two men began to walk towards the door. 'Do you ever hear news of Judas?' he asked nonchalantly. Simon still did not know what had happened to his son.

Peter stopped and covered his mouth with his hand. 'Did you not hear?' he asked 'Oh, you poor man. All this time not knowing.' Peter explained what had happened to Judas as he knew it. How he had been found hanged. Simon just stood there staring at Peter. Then years of guilt and remorse began to erupt. He let out a long painful cry as if he had just been stabbed. He was very distressed and turned away. It was time for tears of a different nature now. Such an overwhelming conflict of thoughts and emotions nearly broke his troubled heart. Peter tried to comfort him, but all he really wanted was to be left alone. He had been feeling so happy and now he felt utterly miserable.

'It's all my fault. But I never thought...' he sobbed uncontrollably. 'It's me who deserves to die.'

Peter sensed his mood and sat him down and tried to comfort him. But he realised a closer friend would be more use at a time like this. 'I will get Aeneas. I think he is what you need right now my friend.' He rose and turned to leave. As soon as he opened the door there was Aeneas standing there looking very concerned. He had heard the cry and wondered what could possibly have happened.

Peter told Aeneas, who immediately went in to Simon to comfort him, and the two men sat there for some time together.

It was the time of day that Cornelius usually returned from his duties. There was a noise of servants scurrying around in the atrium, welcoming Cornelius home. He breezed in joyfully and everyone rose to greet him. Peter stepped forward and explained that there were another five visitors who had come that day. Cornelius didn't seem at all concerned and greeted his new guests enthusiastically. He was particularly excited to meet Aeneas, about whom he had heard so much, and wanted to hear, first-hand, all about his experience of healing.

He was so excited to have yet more believers in his home that he decided they should have a special celebration to welcome everyone. Servants were quickly despatched to buy provisions from the market before it closed and there was much activity and excitement in the house. It was a wonderful evening and Cornelius had gone out of his way to make sure that there was nothing on the menu that might offend anyone.

Cornelius was so excited and consumed with organising the party that Peter felt constrained to interfere on account of Simon. A party would be the last thing he would want at this time. But the longer he dithered the more difficult it became to say anything. So, for the sake of the rest of the group who had responded enthusiastically, he let it be.

One of Peter's disciples was a skilled musician. He had composed some songs of praise to Yeshua. He was also well acquainted with traditional Jewish music. After dinner they sang and danced to traditional music. Cornelius loved singing, although he wasn't that good at it, but his newfound joy in the Lord had stirred a desire in him to sing. At one point he asked to sing a solo. Everyone politely applauded at the end, but more out of respect for who he was than for his musical talent.

Cornelius was another larger-than-life character like Peter, and the two of them got on well right from the first time they met. He was the sort of person who stood out in the crowd anyway, but since the Holy Spirit had fallen on him, he was on fire for the risen Lord. He had a new purpose in life and never missed an opportunity to extoll the good news to those he met; the good news that Yeshua had risen from the dead and was alive and living.

Since his experience when the Holy Spirit had fallen on him, he and all his household had become quite a large group of believers. Each evening they would get together, meeting at his home for prayer and inviting in their friends and relatives and sharing with each other their individual stories about what Yeshua had done in their lives. In next to no time, they had outgrown Cornelius' home as more numbers were added, and soon they had to split in two, with one meeting being held at the house of one of Cornelius' friends. Then, once a week, they would get together on the first day of the week at a different location where they had more space. So Cornelius was no stranger to large numbers of people descending on his home to meet and talk about Yeshua.

Because Peter was still with them, Cornelius could invite a much wider circle of his friends and acquaintances to hear the good news at their weekly get-togethers. The fact that they had barely been meeting for more than a month didn't strike anyone as unusual. They were all so caught up in this outpouring of the Holy Spirit that every eye was focussed on Yeshua and his teaching, even though to any casual observer he didn't actually appear to be visibly present!

Cornelius, ever the planner and organiser had already asked Aeneas if he would stay on with them to share his story at their weekly meetings. He had ambitious plans to invite all his fellow centurions and many others in the Legion, as well as people he knew in Herod's civil administration based in Caesarea.

For Simon that night, the idea of joining in a party was the last thing he felt like doing. In fact, he had not joined in the dancing, partly because he wasn't that fond of dancing, but more particularly because it reminded him of his days in Kerioth. He had often watched Judas, as a young teenager who loved music, throwing himself wildly about doing some of the more traditional dances. He was very fond of the traditional side of his culture. But now Simon just didn't feel like celebrating. Instead, he took himself off into the garden alone.

It was a warm evening. He had left the leather case containing the scrolls propped up in a corner of his room covered by his cloak. As he was sharing a room with so many others, there were clothes and bags all over the floor. He had chosen a discreet corner away from harm's way. Outside he took in the Caesarean night sky, ablaze with stars, the night air filled with the sweet evening scent of herbs and flowers from the garden. It reminded him a little of the garden beneath his window in the Old Refectory in Jerusalem and he wondered if he would ever go back there. Somehow, he felt it was unlikely.

Chapter 21

# RECONCILED

It was still quite noisy, even away from the house.

A little gravel path led down to a small gate at the bottom of the garden. Approaching, he saw that a sentry was on guard duty. 'Can I get down to the sea from here?' he enquired. The sentry looked a little apprehensive. He was not supposed to leave his position without authority, and he was uneasy about letting one of the house guests just wander off in the night without an escort.

'If you wait here, sir, I will just go and get a relief for the gate and then I can escort you personally down to the sea,' and he turned to go up to the house.

'Oh, don't worry about that,' said Simon reassuringly, 'I can take care of myself, and besides this hasn't been a very happy day for me. I received some sad news and I just want to be on my own,' Simon could see the sentry wasn't entirely happy. Perhaps he was concerned he might drown. 'I am a good swimmer,' he added jokingly.

The sentry thought for a minute, and seeing that Simon was a mature man and not carrying anything valuable, he decided to let him pass. 'Don't be too long, sir. I suggest you stick to the path and if you get lost or have any difficulty, I'll listen out for you. Just give me a shout.' He swung open the gate and let Simon pass with the parting words, 'Don't go near the sea, sir. The tides are pretty strong here and we have had people drown. Even good swimmers, sir.'

Simon thanked the sentry and set off down the well-defined moonlit path leading to the sea. As he did so, he thought he heard something move in the grass to his left. He turned to see what it was. Even in the moonlight, he couldn't see anything. Looking back at the house to make sure he had his bearings, he saw that it was well lit with lanterns. The sentry was watching so he waved to him, but he didn't respond.

As he turned back towards the sea, he thought he saw a small light a short distance off to the left about a hundred yards away. He thought nothing of it. Probably fishermen getting ready to go out fishing or another sentry out on patrol. This part of Caesarea was well guarded by the military presence, so he had nothing to fear.

The foreshore was covered in knee-high scrub vegetation over shallow dunes, so the path was easy to follow. Eventually it opened out onto the beach. He checked his bearings again and the house was still clearly visible. It was a beautiful evening and he stopped to admire the glittering moonlight reflecting off the sea. Breakers gently folded on to the sand, rumbling up the beach against a light evening breeze. He wandered a little further on and sat down on a rock protruding from the sand.

It was a time to be alone with his thoughts. Thoughts of Judas particularly, but he also thought of Yeshua. Such moments allow the mind to wander, and his mind began to imagine what he would say if the risen Yeshua were to appear to him there and then. More to the point, what would he do? All alone on the beach he actually felt very close to Yeshua, and he wondered what Yeshua would look like in his resurrected form. The last time he saw him he was dead on the cross, just hanging there. It was gruesome and awful. It was hard to imagine what he would look like now. What would he be dressed in? Would his voice sound the same?

Then, without warning, he had a sense that he was not alone. It made the hair stand up on the back of his neck. He had a powerful feeling that someone was very near him. He didn't dare look around. He became transfixed sitting there. He waited, half expecting Yeshua to step out into the moonlight. His heart was pounding, and he could hardly breathe.

Shockingly and without any warning he felt a hand over his mouth. He tried to cry for help, but the hand suffocated any sound he could have made, and he found himself being violently wrestled to the ground face down. His arms were twisted up behind him with a knee in his back. There were two men. One gagged him so hard he could only just breathe, while the other tied his hands. They tied his feet and began to drag him off along the beach. There they were met by a third man with a lantern. He shone the light in Simon's face, making it impossible for him to recognise his assailant.

'That's him alright!' said the man with the lamp, speaking in Latin but with a thick Jewish accent. 'Did anyone follow you?' he asked.

'No sir, he was alone, no one saw us. Bit of luck him wandering out like that. We saw him speaking to the guard and he was just like you said, sir.' The two men who set on Simon were clearly Latin speaking Romans who had been sent to try and find a way of kidnapping him. Being much older than most of the other house guests, Simon wasn't difficult to identify. His walk down to the beach had played straight into their hands.

'Get him on the cart as quickly as you can!' The man with the Jewish accent whispered urgently. He was keen not to attract any unwanted attention. The two Romans dragged him a few more feet and then they literally picked him up and threw him into the back of the cart face down. One of the men held his head down. Despite a bleeding nose, he could smell the animal in front.

'Go, go!' whispered the man with the Jewish accent. He heard the driver flick the animal with his whip and the cart lurched forward. After a short distance there was more whipping and the animal broke into a trot. Simon bumped about in the back of the cart for what seemed like about twenty minutes.

Eventually, the cart rumbled over some flagstones with an echo that sounded as if they were going under an archway and into an open courtyard. His head was still pinned face down to the floor of the cart and he could see nothing. He had no idea which way he had travelled, but he estimated he had gone about one and a half miles. He could hear voices. Some were in Aramaic and others in Latin.

They dragged him out of the cart and down some steps into a building and along a dark corridor into a musty smelling room.

He couldn't see the faces of his captors, but soon they were gone, taking their lantern and locking the door behind them. Simon lay there listening in pitch black darkness, still trussed up. He rolled over. Thankfully his gag had worked loose enough to allow him to breathe a little through his mouth. His nose was still partially blocked by congealed blood.

He got the impression he was below ground somewhere, but who had abducted him and why? More to the point, what were they going to do to him? There was nothing he could do but wait and see.

Ever since he evaded capture in Jerusalem, this was the nightmare he had been living with. Caiaphas was a determined man, and he didn't like being given the slip. He had a reputation for getting what he wanted and so far, he hadn't got what he wanted with Simon Ish Kerioth.

He lay there on his back for about fifteen minutes, wondering if he was going to have to spend the entire night tied up. The room smelt damp and the floor was filthy. There didn't appear to be a window of any sort, and with the door closed the atmosphere was airless and claustrophobic.

A few minutes later he heard some voices and his captors returned to his cell. They untied him and stripped him bare, wrenching his gag off roughly. His hands were numb and his mouth dry and painful. 'There's nothing here. Must have dropped it somewhere,' one of them said, leaving him naked on the floor. 'Don't even think about calling for help or you'll spend the night tied up! Got it?' he threatened.

'Who are you and what do you want?' Simon asked, but to no avail.

The door banged shut and he heard the lock trip over. Once more, he was alone. He dressed and propped himself up against the wall. He guessed they were looking for the scrolls, which he would normally have been carrying, but not tonight.

Simon drifted in and out of sleep until the morning. He woke up feeling thirsty and tired. He was not about to make a search of the cell in the dark for water. He could smell that it had recently been used for human habitation, and with no latrine or washing facilities the smell was distinctly unpleasant.

Although there was no light in his cell, there was a faint glimmer coming from under the door, which must have been finding its way from a lamp down the passage.

With the advent of dawn, the light took on a new colour as the sun rose, and he watched as it grew in strength. He felt strangely peaceful, as if he was not alone. Now, as he watched the light grow brighter under the door, it felt as if Yeshua was present with him. As the light under the door was growing, Yeshua's light was beginning to grow within Simon. It was not something he had been seeking but he realised that he had been in a very dark place and this marvellous light had crept in under the door of his life. Yeshua had come looking for Simon, not the other way around. It was a testament to G_d's profound love that an old man had to be locked in a cell in the dark to realise what was happening to him. It actually didn't matter that the light was so small because he knew it would grow, just as Yeshua's love would grow in him.

Sitting in that dark and damp cell his thoughts dwelt on his Messiah. He thought about how Yeshua's last night was also spent in a dark cell and as he thought about him, he wondered if this would also be his last night. As he thought about it, he found himself praying softly in a way he had never experienced before. He wasn't sure what he was praying. It was as if someone else was doing the praying in him. Things too marvellous to speak about. Things of the most inner soul. The Holy Spirit of Yeshua gently speaking in him and through him. He let the Spirit remain, rejoicing in his own spirit at what his Lord had done for him.

He could feel a wonderful warmth in that cold cell. He was definitely not alone. He had no idea where he was on earth, but he knew where he was in Yeshua. He figured out his destination would be Jerusalem and who knows what, but it didn't matter anymore. Despite all that he had conspired to do in the past, he was becoming aware that the surpassing grace that G_d had shown him in saving him meant so much more than any rescue from his earthly predicament. His life, his purpose, the scrolls and even his end were now in Yeshua's hands.

As he lay there, his thoughts began to turn towards his friends, who would be waking up to a new day without him. He felt a deep concern for the unfinished work that still lay propped up in the corner of his room. What would happen to it now? He found himself repeating the words to Yeshua. The only hope for the future was now in Yeshua's hands. He began to speak out his concerns to him in a new way. It was from his heart, and it gave Simon a feeling of comfort in that it was no longer up to him to ensure the outcome of what was going to happen next.

Less than two miles away, the sun rose over the back of the villa where Cornelius, Peter, and the followers of Yeshua were staying. The household arose to celebrate another day. There was a time of prayer held in the atrium. Songs were sung and a passage from Psalm 118 was read. It was a wonderful way to start the day. At breakfast Peter broke bread and blessed it before handing it round. He stood there with the present company at his feet, intending to say a few words of encouragement about the reading. He was planning to speak about verse 22 of the Psalm, about the stone that the builders rejected becoming the corner stone in the person of Yeshua, and to tell them about the scrolls, the evidence that had been collected to condemn Yeshua, which now stood to become the principle evidence for his defence. But as he looked around the room for Simon, he couldn't see him.

'Where's Simon?' he asked softly. Everyone looked around the room, but he was absent.

'Maybe he has gone for a walk,' suggested Aeneas.

'I saw him go out last night, but I don't recall seeing him return,' reported Silvanus.

Cornelius stood up immediately. 'Guard!' he called out. A soldier immediately entered the atrium. 'Who was on duty last night?' he asked.

'I was, Sir.'

'Did you see a man leave the premises last night?'

'Sir, a man did leave through the garden gate, he was alone and asked if he could go for a walk, Sir.'

'Did you let him go alone?'

'I offered to go with him, but he insisted on being on his own. I think he said he'd had a bereavement, sir.'

'Did you see him return?'

'Er, no sir.'

'Which way did he go, man?'

'He headed down the path towards the sea sir, I did warn him about the currents sir.'

Cornelius, for all his newfound love, was not best pleased but tried not to show it in front of everyone; this was not the place or time for an interrogation.

'Take Augustus and go now and search for him. Make a detailed search of the beach and report back as soon as you can.' The soldier left immediately with his companion. They searched the area thoroughly, but the tide had covered the evidence of the struggle the night before. All they found were some cart tracks leading from the beach out onto the road. There was no sign of Simon.

Reporting back, they entered a house where the mood was noticeably different. Up until then it was a household of joy, but now the mood had turned to solemn silence and prayer. Despite a thorough search of all the possible places in the city where he might have been taken, no one knew or had seen anything.

After a few days, the search had to be abandoned. Cornelius had his suspicions as to what might have happened, but even his intelligence, which was well grounded, failed to produce a single lead. Money usually talked, but it could just as easily be used to shut people up and, on this occasion, no one spoke a word.

Aeneas and his friends stayed on before returning to Lydda. They left when Peter and his disciples returned to Jerusalem. As they packed up to leave, a cloak, travelling bag and underneath it, an old, well-travelled, cylindrical shaped leather case were found in the corner of one of the rooms. They realised they were Simon's belongings. It was a sad day anyway but finding

Simon's possessions made it even worse. They asked Peter what they should do with them.

Peter's eyes lit up. He had been told that Simon went everywhere with his scroll case and had assumed the scrolls had gone with him. It had become a standing joke, but this time he had left it behind. He cradled it in his arms like a child who had been lost and found. He guessed Simon had been abducted to take possession of the scrolls and that he would never see them again, but that was not to be! 'I think I'll take care of that,' he said with a smile. He had made Simon a promise which he intended to keep.

Peter handed the other possessions to Aeneas. All Simon's family were deceased, and Aeneas was the only true friend Simon had ever known. Aeneas took them with eyes full of tears. Everyone embraced each other, filing silently out of Cornelius' house before departing. It had been a very special time, now bludgeoned with great sadness.

So what had become of Simon? Had his grief driven him to take his own life like Judas?

When Peter arrived back in Jerusalem, he stayed with Mary, the mother of a young man called John Mark. Mark had a lucky escape during the betrayal of Yeshua, when he nearly got himself arrested. He had escaped naked from his captors as he was only wrapped in a linen sheet. Peter often stayed with them, and they became the best of friends.

John Mark was well educated, speaking several languages. He was fluent in Greek and Latin and could write proficiently in both as well as his native Aramaic. When Peter showed him the scrolls, he became utterly fascinated by them. He read and re-read them and asked Peter if he could help him write an account of Yeshua's life and ministry. Peter agreed, but it would be some time before their account would be circulated and much would occur to threaten the outcome. In time, the project was completed, and quickly became a vital source document to which others referred when writing their own accounts.

As for Simon Ish Kerioth, no one ever saw him again. There was a rumour that he was being held in detention somewhere in Jerusalem, but no amount of enquiry produced any evidence. No charges were ever levelled against him, and no trial ever recorded. Some said he had escaped and was living in exile, others that he had walked into the sea at Caesarea and taken his own life like his son, Judas. As for Peter, he never let on where the scrolls came from.

Despite all the rumours, the truth about what really happened to Simon Ish Kerioth would remain a mystery. All that would ever be recorded about him was that he was the father of Judas Ish Kerioth.

© Colin Rank
1<sup>st</sup> September 2019

# POSTCRIPT

*"Truth is ever to be found in simplicity,*
*and not in the multiplicity and confusion of things."*
Isaac Newton

Some years ago, my old Bible began to fall apart. So, when my mother asked me what I wanted for my birthday, I asked her for a new leather-bound edition of the same version. The copy she found came with the words of Jesus printed in red. Having the words of Jesus in red tends to focus the mind on *when* Jesus is speaking and *what* he is saying.

As the years went by and I read and re-read the Gospel narratives, I noticed that in the Synoptic Gospels (the first three Gospels), whenever Jesus was speaking, the scribes and Pharisees would often be present and the content of what he was saying would frequently be controversial to them.

There are passages that place him out in the countryside and some by the Sea of Galilee speaking to large numbers of followers, yet there are more frequent passages that place him in the synagogues or in the Temple. He is often healing on the Sabbath or saying things that contravene the accepted convention of his day. It seemed odd to me that anyone sitting at Jesus' feet so to speak, a follower or a disciple of his, and recording what he was saying would focus so predominantly on his controversial statements. If I had been taking notes and recording his speech or recalling it afterwards, and I wanted to portray Jesus in the true light of being 'The Good News', I would have concentrated more on the meat of what he was teaching and not so much on the controversial clashes with the authorities.

In stark contrast is the type of teaching and miracles recorded in John's Gospel, particularly the dialogue recorded at the Last Supper, including Jesus' spoken prayers. Here we are given much more insight into the deeper teaching relating to the Christian life. According to his closing remarks at the end of John's gospel, he makes it clear that the record set down is John's own.

The accepted wisdom is that the Gospel of Mark was the first Synoptic Gospel to have been written. Matthew's account is thought to have been written largely from Mark but expanded on, and Luke likewise but with some additional material from an unknown source. The Gospel of John is totally different and follows an independent theme.

Compared to the other Gospels, John's Gospel is particularly notable for both the stories it leaves out, as well as for the extra stories it includes. For example, the first recorded miracle at the wedding in Cana and the raising of Lazarus are unique to John's account. Both are worth a special mention because they appear to have been attended by Jesus' disciples. It seems a mystery to me that the raising of Lazarus, which was such an extraordinary event and which, from the author's own account, became public knowledge, does not even get a mention in the Synoptic Gospels.

Then there are events which one might expect to find in John's Gospel that are missing. For example, the Transfiguration, which is recorded in all three Synoptic Gospels, includes John among a select group of disciples who were present, the other two being James and Peter. Did John feel the Transfiguration was not relevant to his account?

It has been suggested that Peter had a hand in preparing the material for Mark's Gospel, and if he did it might explain why he is the only disciple to speak at the Transfiguration. Curiously, Jesus is not recorded as saying anything, except in Matthew's version. Considering neither Matthew, Luke, or Mark were there, it does suggest that perhaps one of those who were present provided the recorded speech for the Matthew account. However, if it was Peter, why is that the recorded speech of Jesus is not in Mark's account? And if it was John, why did he leave the whole incident out of his own account? Maybe it was James, or perhaps Jesus retold the account to the rest of the disciples?

But the Transfiguration is not the only narrative that has very little of Jesus' recorded speech. The story about the demon Legion is another. This is quite a long and involved story in which one might expect Jesus to have rather more to say than his parting words to the man he has just healed as he is about to get into the boat. Perhaps the person recording those words had remained with the boat or was in one of the other boats accompanying them?

When one compares the treatment of this story with some other stories, the format is very different. For example, when the Pharisees and other leaders are present, there is no shortage of what Jesus has to say, and the same applies when he is turning the accepted wisdom of the day on its head or having a dig at the authorities. Why so much recorded speech in these circumstances?

As I pondered these points I wondered if it might be possible that someone else other than one of the disciples could have been the source of his recorded words in Mark's gospel. Someone who wasn't always present but when he was, he made a careful note of what was being said.

In Mark 1:21-28 Jesus drives out an impure spirit from a man whose outburst is recorded in about 25 spoken words. Jesus responds with just 6 words. The onlookers also have their response recorded word for word in about 20 words. There is nothing unusual about that, except that the story has other information. When you go back to the beginning of the story it starts with Jesus entering the synagogue and 'teaching'. It describes how people were *amazed* at his teaching because he taught as one who had authority and not like the other teachers. I find it remarkable that the author makes a careful note of the exact words used in the deliverance but seems totally disinterested in the teaching, not even the topic. One wonders why the comment is even included. That strikes me as unusual.

There are about six occasions when Mark records that Jesus taught the people, but on only one occasion do we get given the content of his teaching, and that is when he taught them the parable of the sower, which he later explained. This account is very detailed.

On another occasion he returns to Nazareth accompanied by his disciples and enters the synagogue. Many are *amazed* by his teaching and wisdom, but we are still not treated to the content! In Luke we have a similar if not the same visit. But unlike Mark, in Luke's account we are given quite a bit of teaching from the famous passage in Isaiah 61 announcing that the 'Spirit of the Lord is upon me.'

So, I asked myself the obvious question:

Who would only be interested in recording in detail the moments of open conflict with the authorities and not be interested in recording any detail about what Jesus was teaching and why?

It was at that point that the thought occurred to me which led to the process of writing this novel.

Could the principal material for Mark's Gospel have been recorded initially by someone who was more interested in collecting evidence to prosecute Jesus, but as time went on, they began to realise that there was much more to this man than meets the eye? Did the author(s) of Mark's account feel that what had been recorded was so authentic it was sacred and that they didn't want to add anything to it which was merely a recollection or hearsay?

It was an intriguing thought which would go some way to explaining why miracles like the raising of Lazarus are not included, simply because the author of the basic material was not present when it happened. Of course, the solution I have adopted in this novel is just one suggestion. There are other possible alternatives but to me this is the most credible one.

So, I needed a candidate for the role of recorder, and I needed a motive.

It was at this point that I noticed that John, in his Gospel narrative, seldom refers to Judas Iscariot without adding that he is the son of Simon Iscariot. There is no explanation of who Simon was or why John goes out of his way to pointedly and repetitively link Judas with his father Simon. Of course, he might just be distinguishing him from another Judas, but in John 14:22 he deliberately refers to another Judas as '*not* Judas Iscariot'. It is as if there is something about Simon that he thinks will be known to his readers and which might also be contentious. It's as if he is not entirely happy about this man and wants to make sure his readers know he is Judas' father and firmly link him with his notorious son. He might well be unhappy about my suggestion that Simon was the primary author of the Synoptics, and if that had been the case it might account for his response. But that's stretching the imagination! Clearly John is distinctly unhappy about Judas. He is the one who records the most damning comments about him.

In the Synoptic Gospels Judas is mentioned in only two chapters of each gospel, and the first mention is only to list him as a chosen disciple, but in John's Gospel he is mentioned in no less than 5 chapters. Clearly Judas' part in the story of Jesus meant a lot to John. It is John who in John 17 has Jesus speaking to his Father about his ultimate end. Here Judas is referred to by John as 'son of the destroyer' or 'son of perdition' depending on the translation. Quite what John meant is not altogether straightforward. The word 'perdition' only came into the English language in the 14th century from the Anglo-French 'perdicion', a word derived from the Latin 'perdere' to destroy or to waste or to lose. More recently the word has evolved to mean *eternal* destruction, but did John actually mean 'eternal'?

At the time it was spoken by Jesus, Judas was still alive, along with the other disciples. Are we to understand that this man, whom Jesus chose as one of his twelve disciples but who was a devil (Jn 6:70) and unclean (Jn 13:11) was an *unpardonable* sinner? A man who was so deeply upset that Jesus had been condemned that he hung himself? Was he remorseful yet still unrepentant? Was it greed that led him into error? Where did he think his betrayal of Jesus would lead? It's only John who does not mention the unpardonable sin of blasphemy against the Holy Spirit. (Mt 12:32, Mk 3:29 and Lk12:10)

When you examine all the evidence, in the Synoptic Gospels and in John's Gospel, you might be left wondering whether there was room in Judas' final moments for repentance and forgiveness between him and his maker? Whether he got paid the same wage as those who clocked on first thing in the morning? Only G_d knows!

So, after looking at all the evidence, I began to get the idea for a story that explores what is omitted in the Gospels, without contradicting what is there. It took a long time to gather my thoughts together. One thing stood out however, namely that the Gospel narratives are almost as interesting for what they do not say as for what they do.

Should you vehemently disagree with the whole concept behind this novel, please just remember that it is just that, a novel; a fictional story!

You may feel that this is a story which would have been better left untold. I also felt like that, and before I could commit these ideas to paper, I needed to deal with this query which was niggling me. I felt I needed G_d's permission to commit the story to paper. That was until I spent Christmas with my son, and we all went to St Mary's Church in Funtington, West Sussex, on Christmas Day.

As I was preparing myself for worship sitting in the south aisle, the thought returned to me, and I put the question to the Lord. When I had finished my silent time of prayer, I casually glanced at the stained-glass window on my right. It is dedicated to a passage from Revelation 21:5.

There, in very large letters in the centre of the window, was the word "WRITE".

On closer inspection, the passage being quoted refers to the One who sits on the throne, speaking to John about making everything new, and then he instructs him to write it down! It quite took me by surprise, but I concluded that either the Lord likes a good yarn or...

*Funtington Church Window*

ENT HERZ FÜR AUTOREN A HEART FOR AUTHORS À L'ÉCOUTE DES AUTEURS MIA KAPΔIA ΓIA ΣYΓ
UN ΛΙΤA FOR FÖRFATTARE UN CORAZÓN POR LOS AUTORES YAZARLARIMIZA GÖNÜL VERELIM S
CUORE PER AUTORI ET HJERTE FOR FORFATTERE EEN HART VOOR SCHRIJVERS TEMOS OS AU
ZÖINKÉRT SERCE DLA AUTORÓW EIN HERZ FÜR AUTOREN A HEART FOR AUTHORS À L'ÉCO
CORAÇÃO BCEЙ ДУШОЙ К ABTOPAM ETT HJÄRTA FÖR FÖRFATTARE À LA ESCUCHA DE LOS AUT
AUTEURS MIA KAPΔIA ΓIA ΣYΓΓΡΑΦΕIΣ UN CUORE PER AUTORI ET HJERTE FOR FORFATTERE EE
YAZARLARIMIZA GO RE ZÖINKÉRT SERCE DLA AUTORÓW EIN HERZ F
VOOR SCHRIJVERS OS CORAÇÃO BCEЙ ДУШОЙ К ABTOPAM ETT HJÄRTA F

# The author

Born the second child of three with two sisters,
Colin Rank grew up in Sussex and was educated
locally and in Somerset before leaving school at
18. Over 51 years, he enjoyed careers in the food
industry, the motor trade, and finally in farming.
Some consultancy work and charitable work
followed before taking up a position as Chairman
of the Diocesan Board of Finance in Gloucester, a
role he carried for 5 years.
Colin has a wide range of interests, from a love
of aviation, cars, and motorbikes to playing
drums, making films, sailing, and skiing. An
active Christian, he has been a school governor,
a charitable trustee, and a church synod
representative.
Colin is married with three children and 10
grandchildren and spends many happy hours
maintaining the house and garden and mending
broken furniture for others. He loves turning wood
and pottering in his workshop.